ABANDO
THE VOID...

A sudden burst of static on his miniature radio caused him to pause. And in that instant came a flashback—to seven deadly missiles, raining their destructive energy on the planet Onaris from a distance of better than six hundred light years . . . *from clear across the galaxy*. His mind reeled at the immensity of this. Frantically, he put out a call.

"Ananias, I . . ."

No answer.

"Ananias?"

Again no answer. The transferlink, his only tie to the control center of the Galactic Federation, had been abandoned. For the first time Bron was utterly alone . . .

. . . but against what awesome power from the far shores of space?

PATTERNS
OF CHAOS

COLIN KAPP

ace books
A Division of Charter Communications Inc.
A GROSSET & DUNLAP COMPANY
360 Park Avenue South
New York, New York 10010

PATTERNS OF CHAOS

Cover art by Paul Alexander

This printing: May 1978

■

THE NIGHT WAS shattered by a hundred copper candles, pressor beams bearing down, feathering the mighty bulk of a ship on to the center of the city, bruising the very bedrock with resonant thunder. Green and violet, the lace traces of Yagi beams stabbed sharp disruption into the fabric of the buildings, and the quick flick of lasers struck fires that completed the destruction. The city of Ashur on Onaris, razed by the blistering savagery from above, writhed in agony and prepared to surrender. Resistance was suicide—and even acquiescence held no guarantee of survival.

Perhaps it started as a whisper in some white wilderness—the sick spite of a broken body, cradled in cold, crying futility unto a futile wind:

DON'T YOU KNOW THAT
GOD IS DYING?

In the uncertain shadows against a broken wall the figure of a young man lay in fetal position, only partially aware of the devastation raging around him. Such consciousness as he bore was almost entirely consumed by a battle of equally desperate proportions deep within his skull.

Perhaps in the sordid cells of some inhuman inquisition a spirit snapped, the mind mazed not by the searing steel, the nibbling nerve—but by a vaster wound:

DON'T YOU KNOW THAT
GOD IS DYING . . . DYING . . .

The man moaned softly to himself and rose to a sitting position, cradling his face in his hands. A Yagi beam, green and malignant, sliced the end from a nearby building and the area was deluged with falling bricks. He sank back, unable to fight.

Perhaps some maimed martyr, crazed upon the cross, held up his head and cried unto the heavens:

LORD, WHY HAST THOU
FORSAKEN ME?

And was answered never. The ultimate betrayal. The immaculate blasphemy . . .

HAS NOBODY EVEN TOLD YOU?
THEY SAY THAT GOD IS DEAD.

The young man climbed to his feet and started slowly and still unseeing across the littered square. His uncertain path took him nearly into the beam of a probing Yagi, but fate and guesswork diverted his feet. He blundered finally into the wall of a building, recoiling with a bloody forehead to sink

2

again into the timorous shadows of a ruined doorway.

Bron! Bron, for pity's sake, why don't you reply?

He made no answer. The blood from his forehead trickled down his face and ran salty into his mouth. Soon the shock and the pain forced him from his reverie and pressed on him a brutal acceptance of his environment. For the first time he showed an awareness of the holocaust. He looked out across the flickering waste of the tormented city, agony and comprehension filtering across his torn brow.

Bron, for God's sake answer.

The sky flared suddenly green and hideous as the Yagi's beams found and detonated an unknown arsenal. The blast from the explosion damned the building as a sanctuary and only instinct flung him clear. The walls between which he had been sheltering broke apart and the door against which he had pressed his back seconds before was buried deep under a murderous pile of masonry.

Bron, are you receiving me at all?

"I hear you." In clear ground on the square he stopped and forced himself to speak, his voice ragged with undertones of near hysteria. "Where are you? I can hear you, but I can't see you."

Jupiter! The voice was aghast. *No! You have to be joking! Six years and a quarter of the Commando budget were needed to place you where you are—and now you feign amnesia. Bron, you must be joking!*

"I never felt less like joking. I feel sick. Who are

3

you—if you're not imagination?"

Steady, Bron, steady. The big blast must have given you a concussion. You're in a bad way by the sound of things. I had to use the semantic trigger to pull you out of that coma. Is there nothing you remember at all?

"Nothing. I don't know who I am—or who you are. You seem to be speaking in my head. Am I having hallucinations?"

Far from it. This all has a rational explanation. Only your memory is faulty.

"Where am I?"

In the city of Ashur on the planet Onaris. It's under attack by Destroyer ships.

"And you hear me. How do you hear me? Where are you?"

Jupiter! This gets worse. We don't have time for explanations now. First you have to get clear of the square and find a place to rest. I'll explain later if your memory doesn't come back. For the moment you'll have to take what I say on trust.

"And if I don't?"

Don't dare me, Bron. There's too much at stake. If you could remember what you were—and why you are there—you'd know better than to ask the question. Don't make me show you why.

Bron pressed his head into his hands for a full half minute, then straightened.

"Very well. I accept that for the moment. What do you want me to do?"

Move out of the city center. The damage won't be quite so bad on the perimeter. On the other side of the square, as you now face it, is a thor-

oughfare. Follow that until I tell you where to turn. I'll stay with you.

Bron shrugged and followed the instruction, fully aware now of the blistering fury shrieking out of the sky. The ship above was obviously preparing for a landing, ploughing for itself a stabilizing furrow deep in the flesh of the city and savagely eliminating all resistance in the areas surrounding. The relative absence of population in the attack area suggested that the atrocity had not been unannounced. A rising scream to the east told of where yet another spatial dreadnought had decided to make planetfall. Something about the pattern stirred a thread of Bron's memory, but its pursuit eluded him.

Cautiously he picked his way around the edge of the square, finding an unknown talent for making the maximum use of cover against the devastating Yagis. On the far side he found the thoroughfare, once one of the proudest streets of Ashur, now a hulk-lined valley of debris, rimmed with fire.

"You there in my head—are you listening?"

We're always listening.

"How do you listen?"

You've a bio-electronic transducer implanted in your brain. Our equipment is such that we can hear you and speak to you no matter where you go.

Bron absorbed this in silence for a moment.

"Who are you?"

Associates in war. I'm Doctor Veeder. Does the name mean nothing still?

"Yes."

5

It will come to you. And Jaycee and Ananias. We three will be your unseen companions, as we have been in the past. We're all part of the same team.

"What team?"

Special Assignments group attached to the Stellar Commando.

"Ah—"

You recall something?

"I recollect vaguely that I was a Commando— but not here. Terra I remember, Delhi and Europa. I can't recall anything after I left Europa."

That's significant. It was when you left Europa that you started these special assignments. I don't wonder your psyche chose that point to start forgetting . . . Watch out!

Bron moved. The cautionary word and his own instinctive reactions coincided completely. A probing Yagi beam shattered the road surface inches before his feet. The backwash of the flux discharge caught him as he turned, flung him sideways, stunned but relatively unhurt. As the beam sliced on through a yet unbroken colonnade he regained his feet, still shaking with reactive shock.

"You—"

What's the matter, Bron? Are you hurt?

"You saw that Yagi coming. How?" Bron was breathing hard.

Yes, I saw it. I've been trying to break this to you gently, since the relearning of the facts may be something of a traumatic shock in your present condition.

"Spool the riddles! Can you see me, also?"

Not see you—we see through your eyes and we

6

listen through your ears. Day and night we watch and listen to every facet of your experience — Jaycee, Ananias, and myself. That's our job. We can also speak to you and you can't shut us out. Our voices are transmitted directly to your brain. We can do a few other things, too, but we'll go into those later. For now, just follow my instructions. We'll find you a place to rest.

"Very well."

Bron accepted the order with resignation. He was in no fit state mentally to compose an opposition to the voice within his head. Physically he was drained and shaken and desperately in need of rest. He withdrew into himself and followed the instructions mechanically, gradually wending his way into darker corners of the broken streets and away from the focal point of the attack. Finally the voice seemed to cease. Unable to proceed farther of his own volition, he kicked a few bricks from under his feet, sank down to the dusty ground and slept.

"How's Bron now?"

Of the trio, the speaker was the only one in civilian clothes—a simple jet-black sheath which detracted nothing from her femininity. Her strong features were framed by raven hair garnished with self-luminous star-spite spangles. Her full lips rivaled her deep eyes in expressing the contemptuous force of her character.

Her question was addressed to the Medic-commander who turned away from the ranked screens. Dr. Veeder, tall and graying, bore the air of a man who had seen all the worst of life and learned to come to terms with it. Even at the end of his shift at the screens his crisp commando uniform, like his brow, showed no hint of other than authorized creases.

"He's still out, Jaycee, but as far as I can judge it's a perfectly natural sleep." He glanced back at the monitors, examining the pulsing waveforms. "It should be safe to wake him in about an hour."

"Damn him. If he's loused up this project I'll give him such hell he'll wish his mother had been a compulsive virgin."

"Don't climb on his back too heavily when he first wakes. He took a considerable blasting last night. I don't think he'll appreciate the subtlety of your advances—and anyway, this happens to be an exercise in cooperation, not coercion. Ride him the way you usually do and you could very easily put him on the defensive."

"I'd make sure he didn't survive it."

"Agreed—but that's not the point. He has to survive if we're going to get the information we need."

She accepted the point sullenly. Veeder left the screens and reached for his cloak.

"He's all yours, Jaycee. I'm going to get some sleep. Call me if anything unusual happens."

"Engaged." Jaycee slipped into the padded control couch in front of the screens and reached back to draw the curtains partly shut to kill the reflections in the cubicle. Then she began to run a routine check of the controls to ensure that she was familiar with their standing state.

The third member of the trio prized himself loose from the seat of the computer console as Veeder departed. Throughout the preceding conversation he had remained silent, his eyes never once leaving Jaycee. Now he came to stand directly behind her, watching the manifold screens as she trimmed and adjusted their symbolic legends. The bright tabs of his uniform proclaimed him a full Command General and contrasted oddly with his apparent youth, his flaxen hair and pallid complexion. His eyes were curiously bright and he moistened his small, pink lips continuously with a small, pink tongue.

"Doc's right, you know, honey-bitch," he said quietly. "No good lashing into Bron while he's in that state. He won't understand it and he may well go on the defensive. You know what a cuss Bron can be when he turns awkward." He moved forward and leaned against the back of the control couch immediately behind her. His hands hovered only slightly above her shoulders.

"Jet off, Ananias," she said tiredly. "When I want your ideas on how to handle Bron I'll ask for them."

"Sure, honey-bitch. Play it your way. I just thought that as you couldn't have an emotional workout on Bron you might be looking elsewhere for relief." His hands moved on subtly to her bare neck, lingering.

She froze.

"What you askin' for, Ananias? A couple of broken wrists?"

"Honey-bitch—you would not dare try that on

9

me." His voice held an undercurrent of danger.

"In three seconds if you don't take your hands away."

"You're teasing, honey-bitch."

She moved like a cobra, but he anticipated her action and had the additional advantage of operating from a standing position. He broke her hold and pinioned her hands against the couch.

"My God, you tried it, too." He sounded a trifle shaken. "You're a vicious devil, aren't you?"

"You should know, Ananias. You been around long enough."

"Too long, perhaps. That's how I know the time to proposition. You can't live through Bron for very long without breaking."

Momentarily her head turned to the big screen on which, when he was awake, the scene viewed by Bron's eyes was presented. Currently it was blank. The regular rhythm of Bron's breathing and pulse came through a muted speaker against the muffled background rumble of warfare. Various monitors picked up the sounds, separated and analyzed them and presented scan traces of their findings. In electronic representation was displayed as much information about one living individual as it was possible to transmit over the precarious transgalactic bio-electronic transfer link.

A stronger tie, however, existed between Bron, the agent, and Jaycee, his operator. This was the rapport formed by the close coupling of two minds sharing a common experience however differently presented. When agent and operator were psychologically matched to form one complementary personality, the coupling was tightened even further. Sometimes intolerably.

Jaycee faced up and tried to look at Ananias. "You know what that does to me, don't you—livin' through him?"

Ananias kept control of her hands warily. "Sure. That's how I know when you're ripe for an emotional climbdown. Some time you've got to give way—else you're going to crack."

"And you hang around hopin' to collect whatever it is I have to give?"

Her voice was edged like a razor.

"Sure, honey-bitch. I'm a connoisseur. What you have to give is something of an acquired taste. You've a streak of tigerine spite which has no business this side of hell and you have to work it off on somebody. Well—a man could get addicted to that sort of thing."

"And you think you're deservin' of special privileges?"

"I always give good service."

"Look, Ananias, I admit you once caught me off balance after Bron had wound me up. But that's only because you happened to be the first livin' thing down the corridor. It could have been anyone."

There was a long uncomfortable silence.

Then: "You don't mean that, honey-bitch."

"Like hell I don't. When I get that high I don't care what I find as long as it struggles. I don't respond to propositions. I'm not looking for a lover—I'm lookin' for somethin' to help me catch up on a spell of suspended livin'. What I find doesn't need any identity—better he doesn't have any. No matter what, there's only one person I grapple with in the darkness.''

The impasse between them was broken by the urgent summons of telltales on an auxiliary board. Ananias left her and was at the board in an instant.

"Radio room, Jaycee. Report from the Antares transmitters. Come in, Antares. Ananias on line.''

"Hullo, General! There've been new developments on Onaris. To prevent further bloodshed, Onaris radio has just broadcast their government's acceptance of the Destroyers' unconditional surrender terms. Effective opposition to the Destroyers has now ceased.''

"Good. Did the Onarian government put out an appeal for outside help?''

"They started using their FTL transmitters as soon as the Destroyers entered the system. They couldn't expect to be heard except accidentally, of course, if there happened to be a starship within their range.''

"Did you make radio contact with them?''

"No. Our instructions were to the contrary. They could have no idea that our monitoring chain had picked them up.''

"And nobody else answered their call?''

"No one we could detect. Certainly the FTL emergency bands were clear.''

"Keep monitoring the emergency frequencies. If anyone shows sign of answering their appeal— jam them. It's imperative that nobody interferes before the Destroyers have taken what they want and pulled clear.''

''Understood, General. We'll report again if the situation changes.''

Ananias broke the connection and turned back to Jaycee.

''So far everything has gone as planned— except for Bron.'' He frowned at the still vacant master screen. ''The Destroyers have attacked, Onaris has given way, the entire Commando fleet is on yellow alert—and the most expensively prepared Commando agent in history occupies a strategic position in the middle of a raped city, snoring his bloody head off.''

''Not exactly your night, is it, Ananias?''

''Don't grieve for me, honey-bitch. You know I always win in the end. And if I have to wait a little, then the spoils of battle become all the more enjoyable.''

''You're a Godlost weaklin', Ananias. Unprincipled, but a Godlost weaklin'.''

She turned once more toward the screens, this time purposefully studying the traces which told the details of Bron's existence. Ananias moved back behind the couch. He knew better than to attempt to interfere with her now, as she adjusted the microphone and herself and began to reestablish the rapport she had with a sleeping Commando agent half a galaxy away.

''Perhaps in the sordid cells of some inhuman inquisition . . .''

''Damn you for a bitch,'' said Ananias quietly.

II

HIS REST WAS broken by the insistence of a voice.

. . . the mind mazed not by the searin' steel, the nibblin' nerve—but by a vaster wound . . .

"Stop it—stop saying those things."

Get on your feet, Bron. Did you think you deserved a rest day?

Bron stirred in the ruins, cruelly aware of the cold in his bones. The first pink of daybreak washed against the shattered skyline. His head ached and the wound on his temple was stiff with caked blood. With difficulty he rose to his feet, shivering and trying to orient his thoughts.

"You in my mind—you're not the one who spoke to me last night."

15

*God—you should be so lucky as to forget
me—*The voice trailed into spiteful incredulity.
No, Bron. This is Jaycee. Despite the restraints
imposed by the electronic transfer the voice was
clearly feminine. *Doc tells me you took a blastin'.
How much do you remember?*

"Almost nothing. What's all this 'sick spite' and
'God is dying' routine?"

*Hell, Doc was right. You are in a bad way. That
phrasin' is the semantic recall trigger geared into
your subconscious. In any condition of lowered
consciousness, from sleep through to coma, if you
hear that you'll have to respond. The wordin' is
meshed with the hypno-character synthesis which
was impressed on your mind.*

"This gets insaner every minute. What's this
hypno-character thing?"

*An artificial character pattern impressed by
ultra-deep hypnosis. It's the character you have to
be to pass the Destroyers.*

"But I don't even know my own character, let
alone the synthesis."

*The fact you respond to the trigger means the
synthesis is firm. You'll react in the right way to a
proper stimulus, even if you don't understand your
own actions. In a way your memory lapse is fortu-
nate. It'll lessen the conflict between the synthesis
and the real you. God! It's going to be well worth
hearin' you believin' yourself to be a saint, Bron.*

The sarcasm in the voice bit deeply into his
mind.

"Is that what I'm supposed to be, Jaycee—a
saint?"

Rather a sort of electronic Trojan Horse. But get to your feet, we've work to do. The Destroyers have landed three ships around Ashur and their first move will be the imposition of Destroyer Law. That means a complete ban on all movements and absolute obedience to their orders. We have to get you to the place you should have reached last night.

Bron searched his mind for the things he should have known but had lost. "All this is way beyond me, Jaycee. I'd at least like to know the cause for which I'm being martyred."

Ah, that's better—a touch of the old Bron irony. I don't have time to give you much now. Briefly, Cana's Destroyer squadrons have increased the scope of their destruction to a point where they are threatening the Rim Dependencies themselves. We can't police all that volume of space—and they've destroyed thirty-seven known planets in five years. Our only hope of stoppin' them is to trace their baseworld and launch a massive attack on that. That's your job, Bron. The trick is to get you aboard a Destroyer ship in space for long enough to enable us to discover where the baseworld is.

"And that's quite a trick, I imagine."

If only you remembered! It's taken us six years to get this far. First we had to build the giant transmitters in Antares to handle the communications transfer link between us and you over transgalactic distances. It took two years of intelligence work to decide on the best way to attack the problem—and nearly a year developing your cover. And lastly there was you—the kingpin of the whole operation.

"Tell me about me, Jaycee."

Some other time, when I'm feeling really bitchy. Chaos, Bron, that's your forte—the sort of chaos that reaches out and affects everyone and everythin' it touches. It's the one part of your own character we've left unattenuated by the synthesis. It may be the one trait which can bring this mission through.

Bron considered this in silence. Then: "What do I have to do first?"

We've got to fit you into the background so when the destroyers find you, they won't suspect you don't belong. We had a comprehensive cover worked out, but you should have been in position last night.

"Why should the Destroyers want to find me?"

Because you're substitutin' for a man they came to Onaris to find. Look, I'll have to fill in the details as we go. But listen to me, Bron—this is important—play the game exactly as we give it to you and rely on the synthesis for continuity. Don't try any fool stunts of your own—if you do you're certain to get killed. We've lost more than enough men already just placin' you where you are.

"Which way should I go?"

The sky was gradually growing lighter with the muddy grays of dawn and the vaguest hints of color were substantiating the shadows.

Get out on the thoroughfare and get me a few place names. Once we can pinpoint your position

I'll have the computer give us a route. Then find a mirror and let me look at you. You're going to need to be right in character if we're to get away with this.

Bron shrugged and surveyed the broken walls which had given him partial shelter for the night. Part of the building farther back was relatively undamaged and it was to this he turned. The building proved deserted and the haste of the panicky exodus was underscored by the pattern of disorder in the dim rooms and hallways. He finally found a mirror-covered door. He opened and adjusted it to make maximum use of the available light.

"So that's me—"

Don't you even remember what your face is like?

"I couldn't have called it to memory. Do I fit, Jaycee?"

Not good. You'll have to clean that cut on your forehead. We can't risk sepsis this early in the game.

"I'll clean it somehow. Anything else?"

No—except that I can't get used to your looking like a damned angel. That's the psychosomatic effect of the personality synthesis.

"And what do you propose I do about it?" He was irritated by the malice in her voice.

Don't spoil it, Bron. It'll wear off all too soon. No psychosynthesis yet devised could obscure the real you for very long.

He found street names for Jaycee to work on. His wound he cleansed with water he found in a cistern and he brushed away as much of the caked

19

mud and blood from his cloak as he could manage. Then he returned to the mirrored door to study the effect of his ablutions.

He could not remember donning his clothes, but they consisted of a simple cloak of coarse weave and equally spartan undergarments. About his neck hung a well-worn crucifix of gold on a fine gold chain. A Bible in one of the ample pockets of the cloak appeared to complete his worldly possessions.

As Jaycee had said, his face had acquired a pious intensity—it almost shone from the youthful lines. He studied his features carefully, remembering them vaguely, yet not quite sure how different they had been prior to the hypno-synthesis. He was quietly proud of the strength and character he found in the jaw and brow, but something diabolical seemed to lurk behind the eyes—in depths that at once frightened and fascinated him.

When you've finished your Narcissistic orgy I've got the route for you.

Jaycee's voice came so unexpectedly that it made him jump. He had the feeling she had been watching him in the mirror through his own eyes for some time. The tightness of the surveillance irked him. Something deep inside him clawed for freedom, like a wild beast confined in too small a cage. His expression must have given away his unvoiced emotion, for she picked up the thought with uncanny accuracy.

Don't say it Bron. You're going to have to live with me inside you for quite a while. It's a situation I've come to enjoy—bein' underneath your flesh.

"Bitch."

She laughed.

Yes. I'm that, Bron, and most of the other things you've called me in the past. But now you'd better start travelin'. I'll give you spot directions from whatever landmarks we can still identify.

Her instructions directed him toward a region where the receding night was being shredded by the mottled gray-green erosion of refraction-scattered sunlight. Here even Onaris's famous polychromatic dawn seemed smeared with daubs of blood.

The ruins were unnaturally still and apparently devoid of life. Instinctively he felt to release his sidearm. Instead his fingers touched only on the Bible in his pocket; the discovery brought a twist of taut amusement to his lips. He looked at his hands. The nails were satisfactorily long and the muscles and flesh were hard.

He said, "Jaycee, I know what I have to fight with, but what am I supposed to do with the book?"

For once she did not answer, though he felt she was listening. Her silence brought a harsh realization of the seriousness of his situation. On this mission the synthesis and the book were all the weapons he was going to get.

Smoke from still-burning buildings drifted in broad fronts across his path and Bron trod cautiously, fearing that his sudden emergence from a veil of smoke could lead to his being shot by some observer moved too suddenly to action. Nevertheless he obeyed the instruction implicit in Jaycee's directions and kept strictly to the middle of the roadway, making no attempt at concealment.

"It's too damn quiet, Jaycee. Where are all the people?"

Total evacuation, Bron. The Destroyers have imposed an absolute clearance of a five-kilometer radius around each landing site. Turn around in a full circle, will you. I want to take a check on your position.

Bron turned slowly on one heel, following the skyline with his eyes and dwelling on any features of the broken terrain that might be construed as landmarks.

"On course?"

Near enough. Just clear of the Destroyers' five-kilometer perimeter, but still in the evacuated zone. Your main danger is the Ashur police, who may come looking for looters. Stay in the open and keep your hands empty and in view.

"Shouldn't I be going toward the ship?"

You're jokin'! Cross that perimeter and you're a dead man. The only way anyone gets through there is if the Destroyers choose to take him.

"And you think they'll choose to take me?"

We're hopeful. You're to impersonate a key Onaris technocrat. You were due at the Ashur Seminary last night, but the Destroyers struck before we could get you there.

"What the hell would the Destroyers want with technocrats?"

They take anything that's any value to them— brains, slave-flesh, metals. And as many items of higher technology as they can find. That's why they put down an entire fleet. They strip a planet of anything useful they can carry before they destroy it.

"That doesn't make sense, Jaycee."

No, but it's fact.

"Slave-flesh and metals I can understand, but not technocrats. They can surely train enough of their own."

They appear to be concentrating on ones with a certain specialty—authorities on the patterns of chaos. Seems as though Onaris had one of the top men in that field.

"I thought Terra had all the top men."

That's a classical myth. In fact, the reverse is true. When the starships started the Great Exodus from Terra they took an unusually high concentration of very high IQ emigrants with them. It's not rare on a settlement planet to find two or three families still breedin' an almost pure genius strain. Onaris had one family of decidedly genius strain—the Halterns. You're cast as Ander Haltern, direct ninth descendant of Prosper Haltern. Ander's probably one of the galaxy's top men on the patterns of chaos.

"What happened to the original Ander?"

On Terra, cooperating with us. We took him off secretly six months ago. The story's been patched to support your appearance in Ashur just now. By the way, by Onaris custom, one's familiar name is not on official record, so you're still at liberty to call yourself Bron. I advise you to do so. That split-second's hesitation in respondin' to an unac-

customed name could be crucial in an emergency.

Bron suddenly stopped. "Voices, Jaycee."

Where?

"Beyond the smoke in front."

Yes. I hear them now. A police roadblock, I should imagine. Definitely native Onaris-Ashur accent.

"You can hear all that?"

When necessary we can apply a lot more gain to the signal from your ears than you can. You've got to go through there, Bron. Let the synthesis take over your responses. Don't try to override it. If you do you're likely to come out with a few pure Bron-type answers and reactions—and that could lead to a fairly rapid termination of the project.

As he cleared the smoke he could see what had once been a line of stone-clad buildings, now a mere complex wall, castellated by fire and blast. The road continued haphazardly through the ruins and a barrier had been set across the track. On this were posted men in the green uniforms of the Ashur civil police.

"Stay or we fire." The sudden voice was electronically reinforced.

Bron halted. He saw no possibility of avoiding or withdrawing from the encounter. The sand exploded just before his feet, defining a safe distance for his movements. An officer threw a voice amplifier into the intervening space.

"Approach the apparatus and speak."

Bron moved cautiously towards the amplifier, his hands upstretched and his eyes on the unwavering stubs of the weapons centered on his body.

He inwardly saluted the police technique of maintained distance. Even had he possessed his full Commando equipment he could not have hoped to get a gas slug or shock pellet through to the barrier without drawing fire.

"What are you doing in the evacuated zone?" The amplifier impressed the officer's tones with a sinister metallic burr.

"Trying to get out." Bron's natural resistance to authority produced a spontaneous reply that forestalled any answer the synthesis might have prompted. The amplifier carried his words back to echo quickly against the broken walls.

"I see." The amplifier was critical and unamused.

Fool! You askin' to get killed? Jaycee's anger burst in his head so clearly that he found it nearly impossible to believe that the amplifier would not pick it up and hurl her words across the intervening space. *Play it his way, you stupid cretin!*

"You heard the evacuation order last night. You know we dare not offer any resistance to the Destroyers?"

Yes, prompted Jaycee.

"Yes," said Bron.

"Then you know our instructions are to shoot on sight anyone found in the zone. Have you any reason to offer why that instruction should not be carried out?" The men at the barrier sighted their weapons and prepared to fire.

Jaycee's voice was a flurry: *I've checked his rank, Bron. He's a senior enough animal to be able to exercise discretion—and soft as hell, else he*

25

wouldn't bother to talk. Ride the synthesis, damn you!

"I am Ander Haltern, called Bron, late to adopt my residency at the Seminary of the Sacred Relic." With a shock Bron realized that it was his own voice speaking, but the words and the tone were derived straight from the post-hypnotic suggestion. Intrigued, he let his mind and tongue freewheel. "How else can I reach my destination, save through your barrier?"

"Haltern?" There was a moment of consternation among the police at the roadblock, and the amplifier was swiftly muted to mask a hasty conversation. The Haltern name obviously carried a great deal of weight.

The officer spoke again.

"Can you prove your identity?"

"Is that necessary for a Haltern in Ashur?" The synthesis tightened his tone into intolerant sharpness.

"You have a letter of introduction, perhaps?"

"No letter." A temporary anger welled up inside him and he made a mental note of the shortness of Ander's temper. "What does a Haltern want with paper?"

"Then any other means—"

"If you can't take my word, you must come and see for yourself. Here is all I have."

With a savage gesture Bron stripped the cloak from his shoulder and let it fall to the ground. His undergarments followed, and then, completely naked, he stalked back to the edge of the smoke and waited.

Well clear of the amplifier he spoke softly. "Hell, Jaycee, this is weird. It's unnerving not to know how you're going to act until you've done it."

But you see how the synthesis works, Bron. It responds with a complete takeover of your reactions when a direct stimulus such as a question or a situation demands it.

"If it includes an impromptu striptease every time I'm asked for my identity, this is one synthesis that has definitely no future."

Jaycee was highly amused. *There's no tellin' what you may do. Ander Haltern is a highly individual character. But what worries me is your rapid relaxation out of the synthetic character. It suggests the synthesis isn't set any too firmly. I'll have to put Doc on it when he comes on duty.*

The officer, bearing only a sidearm, came forward and turned the clothes over with his foot. At last he found the Bible and picked it up. Then he held out his hand.

"My apologies, Bron Ander Haltern—but you see, we cannot be too careful. These are very critical times." His eyes wandered apprehensively in the direction of the Destroyer ship. His face was almost gray with worry.

Bron dismissed him curtly. "Can you arrange transport to the Seminary?"

"Of course, Bron Haltern. I will see to it immediately."

The officer returned to the barrier and Bron turned back to his clothes. He could hear Jaycee's outward amusement as he retrieved the garments and solemnly dressed.

27

It's just occurred to me. Jaycee was triumphant.
*Perhaps that's how you're supposed to use the
book, Bron. You take off your clothes and sulk.*

He said, "Damn you, Jaycee," contriving not to
move his lips and in a mere breath of a voice which
the amplifier could not possibly pick up. Jaycee
responded with a peal of laughter.

"You heard that?" asked Bron quietly at the
next opportunity.

*If I hadn't—I'd have guessed. But you don't
need to vocalize. We can pick up subvocal speech
just as well. You should be able to communicate
with us in full view of other persons without their
being aware of it.*

"You've got all the damn answers, haven't
you?"

*More than you're aware of, Bron. And on this
assignment I've got you dancin' like a puppet,
because you don't remember just how sharp some
of those answers are.*

THE SCUDDER PLACED at his disposal was a typi-
cal heavy-duty vehicle, brutally functional and
highly articulate. Under cover of the jet scream
and out of direct sight of the driver, Bron practiced
subvocal communication.

"Can you read me, Jaycee?" The action was no
more than thinking the words and allowing the
muscles of his throat to perform their customary
actions but without the aspiration necessary to
produce a sound.

Loud and clear, Bron.

"What was it about the book that convinced him I'm Haltern?"

I think because it's an old Terran Authorized Version—very rare on a dependency world. Only an intellectual like Haltern could be expected to understand it.

"Bit of a queer bird, this Haltern character."

But brilliant. He's a master syncretist— probably one of the best alive today.

"What's a syncretist?"

One who works across the channels of scientific specialization rather than along them. To qualify for mastership you need at least ten honors degrees in unrelated subjects and the proven ability to think freely across the lines of the various disciplines as well as with them.

The scudder banked swiftly and Bron, restraining an instant of vertigo from sudden awareness of the unexpected height they had attained looked down at the vast edifice below them.

"What's that, Jaycee?"

Ashur Seminary. More correctly, the Seminary of the Sacred Relic of Ashur. That's where the Destroyers will expect to find you.

The scudder burned its way down through the clear air of the morning and drove to an unpolished finish before the great portals. Bron Ander Haltern alighted, obeyed the synthesis-keyed instinct which forbade him even to acknowledge the driver's presence and ascended the great steps of the Seminary. As he did so he felt the mantle of the synthetic character closing around him, entrapping him in the shadowy web of somebody else's mores and reactions. Again the beast that was in him clawed out piteously for freedom.

Nobody awaited him. The vestibule led to a corridor and then to a farther door. Beyond this he found a vast and vaulted hall lit only by the sunlight entering through strangely stained and patterned windows. He stopped suddenly, entranced by the space and unity of the edifice. The great columns that rose to support the beautiful roof were clustered with carved figurines and statuettes depicting scenes which casually had no meaning for him. The walls were similarly complex and ornate, obviously endowed with the same rich symbolism.

The synthesis guided his feet across the floor and down the central aisle between stone blocks arranged as though for seats. At the far end, between white alcoves set into the wall, stood a bare dais. Behind it was a shield emblazoned with the sun-disk symbol of Ashur and centrally in the shield, nailed cruciform, hung the sacred relic—a replica of a small, brown, furry quadruped. Around the shield hypnotic stereo-color tablets spelled out the single word:

GLADLY

"Is this some kind of church, Jaycee?"

Some kind. But not the sort you find on Terra. Not quite that sort of religion either—though they do claim their God is the same.

Bron turned and studied more closely the

figurines on the columns closest to him. He heard Jaycee's sharp intake of breath.

Move closer, Bron. This is interestin'.

"What is it? A monument to De Sade?"

No. An expression of faith. Mortification of the body for the edification of the soul. In the Seminary the cultivation of mind and spirit is all. The body is regarded merely as a vessel of atonement for the weaknesses of the other two.

"Jaycee, that's sick."

It's their way of life. The columns are supposed to depict the classical two hundred and fifty-six modes of penance for weakness.

"After some of those penances there wouldn't be anything left to be weak with."

Subvocalize, Bron. There's someone coming.

Bron scanned the hall swiftly, but no one was yet in sight. His gaze fell again on the sacred relic, whose button-bright and twisted stare suddenly typified the distorted philosophy portrayed by the figurines. The act triggered something in the hypnosynthesis and against his conscious will he dropped to his knees, hands clasped before him, in an attitude of prayer and supplication.

The footsteps closed behind him.

"Ander Haltern?"

"The same." Bron rose and turned to face the questioner.

"What will be your familiar?"

"Bron."

The preceptor—the hypnosynthesis identified the other's function—was lean, gray, ascetic and unwelcoming. "We expected you yesterday, Bron Ander Haltern. How do you answer?"

"Ashur was destroyed by the raiding and I nearly with it."

"You allowed the trivia of the times to come before your duty?"

"Trivia? You damn—" Bron overrode the acquiescent synthesis.

Steady, Bron.

"Bron Haltern, having achieved mastership, you have the privilege of choosing your own penance for absence. What do you offer?"

"What do I answer, Jaycee? The synthesis gives me nothing." Subvocally he could form the words faster than he could have spoken.

Stall him. This wasn't programed. I'm contactin' Ander.

"Ashur is nearly in ruins," said Bron aloud. "The Destroyers are in control. Outside these walls nobody has right of movement or even right of life. Do you still demand penance from one detained by such events?"

"Bron Ander Haltern." The preceptor's face was grave. His eyes were tinged with a depth of irrationality. "You disappoint me. That is not the reaction one has learned to expect from a Haltern. Come, make your offer—or I shall impose one of my own."

The shirt, Bron.

"The shirt," said Bron.

The preceptor's eyes widened abruptly and his jaw dropped. "Forgive me! I meant no disrespect to the Halterns. There is no need—"

The synthesis swung Bron wrathfully. "Are you questioning my decision, Preceptor?"

"Of course not." The preceptor's eyes mirrored agony and embarrassment. "It's just that the act does not warrant such a level of penance. I must ask you again, are you sure you're prepared to accept the shirt?"

"Gladly." The word rose spontaneously from the synthesis.

The preceptor shrugged resignedly. "Very well. I shall conduct you to your cell. The shirt will be delivered to you there."

Bron followed the preceptor out of the hall by a minor door, then through a series of corridors, each similarly ugly and depressing with a severity of line which made no concession to the human need for contrast and relief. The occasional doors were dark, square and massive, with small, high, shuttered windows.

"Jaycee, this is more like a prison than a seminary."

On Onaris there's little to choose between them. Education is inseparable from religion and religion from austerity and disciplined penance. The only thing about the system that stands in its favor is that it produces some remarkably good scholars. Twisted but brilliant.

"I can imagine. And what the hell's the shirt?"

Don't know. It was Ander's idea. He seemed to think it appropriate to the crime. He's getting quite a kick out of the idea.

The preceptor reached a door and halted. The proximity lock responded unhesitatingly to his fingers and the heavy wood swung open. Bron, though accustomed to a lifetime of utilitarian Commando accommodation, stood appalled. The cell he was invited to enter was a featureless stone box. The only attempt at furnishing was the provision of a solitary coffin-sized slab of cut white stone, which presumably had to serve as table, chair and bed. There was nothing else at all.

A solitary eye of unalterable light stared down harshly from the ceiling. The aperture through which it entered was encircled by the gilded message:

GLADLY

The preceptor was watching his face, but Bron managed to remain impassive.

"In a few minutes, Bron Haltern, I will send you the shirt. I suggest you don it immediately, then you will not be unduly late in conducting your first tutorial."

"Is the penance then not to wait until the evening service?"

"No. You have earned greater respect than that. I think your absolution will be more perfect if the work of the shirt is well advanced by the time you bear witness to the assembly."

Under the influence of the synthesis, Bron bowed his head and waited until the preceptor had departed.

"That man's not only a sadist, Jaycee, he's also quite mad. He took in absolutely nothing of what I told him about the destruction of Ashur. His world begins and ends in a small closed circle of Seminary rites. How long do I have to stay here?"

Not long, I guess. The Destroyers always know where to look for the people they want. They must put in some damn good intelligence work before they strike.

"Am I the only one they're looking for?"

We think so. They'll otherwise take mainly slave-flesh. They're obviously colonizin'. Human flesh is a lot cheaper and more versatile than machinery on an undeveloped world.

"Interesting point. The fleshships were not unknown even in the days of Terran space colonization."

Bron broke off as a knock on the door heralded the arrival of a student bearing the shirt. The student slipped the garment from its filmy wrap and left it on the slab. As he passed and bowed, his eyes bore a look compounded both of admiration and profound sympathy.

Bron examined the shirt cautiously. It clung to his fingers as though each fiber of its wool-like texture were possessed of microscopic barbs. With swift decision he stripped and donned the garment—and momentarily its hugging softness was almost luxurious. Its elasticity drew it smoothly over the contours of his body. A few seconds later he was genuinely praying, perhaps for the first time in his life.

In something akin to mortal panic he tried to tear the shirt away from his body, but the myriad barbs of the fine, white fibers were firmly engaged in his flesh. There was no way of removal save that of tearing away the skin. The burning itch and panic drove him to the verge of hysteria before he managed to clamp a bold composure on his reasoning.

"Jaycee, this is diabolical—"

Jaycee laughed. *It's apparently the modern equivalent of the pilgrim's hairshirt. Contemplation, concentration, and sufferin' enrich the mind and ennoble the spirit. And let's face it, Bron, both your mind and your spirit were long overdue for somethin' drastic. I'm quite lookin' forward to the improvement.*

"Damn you for a bitch, Jaycee. One day I'll make you regret that."

A knock sounded at the door. It was the student again.

"Mastership Haltern, sorry if I disturb your devotions. The preceptor requires me to conduct you to the syncretics unit."

"It's no disturbance," said Bron. "I've already made my dedication clear."

Outside the door the youth put his knuckles to his forehead. "You may lean on my arm if you wish, Mastership." His eyes strayed to the shirt, the collar of which showed still above the cloak.

"Thank you, no." Bron declined as the synthesis demanded he must, but from the look in the youth's eyes he knew that the shirt was infamous.

As he walked, Bron could hear Jaycee cataloguing the way. His own consciousness was almost entirely absorbed by the unremitting and painful awareness of the shirt of penance and he was in no condition to master detail. At the door of the

Syncretics unit the student saluted with knuckles to forehead as if in momentary prayer, then departed. Bron touched the proximity lock. After a few seconds' trial the lock responded and he entered the laboratory to give his first-ever tutorial in syncretics.

This time he was impressed. The array of teaching and computing equipment must have cost a fortune. His audience of a hundred, all working in solitary cells, had instant on-line access to the computer as well as real-time monitoring of their own responses. The performance-analysis display panel was a masterpiece of ingenuity and enabled him to correct in seconds the failure of a student to grasp a single point or a single word.

Faced with a specific demand, the stored knowledge in the character synthesis produced all the information he needed. Yielding to the pressures of the synthesis, he allowed his hands to set up channels and controls, not properly understanding his actions until the instant they had to be performed. Then, as he followed the movement of his fingers, he began to understand the instruments before him. His lecture, too, came readily to mind and he spoke first and comprehended later.

Such concentration served to divert his attention from the shirt, but the irritant pain of such an intimate and widespread penetration of the skin was a distraction that permitted him only two states of mind—extreme concentration and abject despair. Moreover his body was reacting violently to the attack with an allergic rash that spread soon to his face and hands and produced an unwholesome puffiness around his eyes.

"Jaycee, this shirt is killing me. Ask Ander how I get the damn thing off."

I already did. Short of extensive surgery there seems no way of removin' it prematurely. The fibers are histamine sensitive. When the allergic reaction raises your body histamine to a sufficient level they will quit of their own accord.

"And for God's sake—how long will that take?"

Depends on the susceptibility of the individual. Could take up to thirty-six hours.

"I see," said Bron grimly. "Have you asked friend Ander what proportion of its wearers die of shock?"

Yes. About ten percent, Bron. If we'd known earlier we'd never have let you put it on.

"Whose side is Ander on?"

Ours apparently. He said the choice of the shirt was to keep you truly in the character of a Haltern. We overlooked the fact that most of the Haltern descendants are mad.

The tutorial lasted five hours, after which Bron returned to his cell. Agonizing though his hours in the tutorial had been, the work had at least partially taken his mind off the shirt. The leisure period offered no such distraction. The allergic reaction of his body was assuming alarming proportions. Muscles in his arms and legs were beginning to react with pain and stiffness which told of the spread of toxins throughout the bloodstream. Occasionally he thought he detected the first fringes of delirium in his brain.

For want of alternative, Bron lay painfully back

on the stone slab and let the bright, unwinking eye
of the solitary light glaze his deliberately unblink-
ing eyes. By varying the range of his vision he
could focus on the legend, GLADLY, or on the
point-source of light or past both to infinity. As he
neared the auto-hypnotic state he experienced
slow alternations of light and darkness until finally
he drifted into sleep.

  *. . . in the sordid cells of some inhuman inquisi-
tion a spirit snapped . . .*

  "Spool it, Jaycee! What's up?"

  Knock on the door, Bron. Two men outside.

  "Damn! I can't go on much longer, Jaycee. If
this thing doesn't give up soon, I've had it."

  *Doc's all but taking Ander apart tryin' to find out
what the shirt's made of. The job isn't easy because native Onaris biology is obviously a field of
its own.*

  Bron swung his feet painfully to the floor and
attempted to stand. The stiffening ache in his joints
at first defied his efforts, but gradually he persuaded his limbs to give him the necessary support. Like a sick man, he stood.

  The two men were dressed differently from
either himself or from the students. Their light-
yellow tunics were obviously designed for ease of
movement.

  "Mastership Haltern, it is time for you to take
the place of witness at the evening assembly."

  The synthesis flashed sharp disapproval into
Bron's mind. "Since when was it the custom to
escort to a penitent to his place?" The phrase was
pure Haltern intolerance.

"The preceptor insists—as an assurance of spiritual discipline."

"Discipline comes from within not by imposition. The preceptor overreaches himself. I shall make my own way."

The wardens appeared momentarily uncertain of their position. Bron took advantage of the fact and steeled himself to walk ahead, shored up primarily by the synthesis-generated anger which fumed at the indignity of having a man's most private hour of fortitude supervised by wardens.

He entered the church and crossed to the center aisle, turning toward the sacred relic behind the dais. Some compulsion greater than his own will forced him to kneel and look upward at the creature's twisted stare. His knuckles sought his forehead. After several minutes thus he attempted to stand, but his stiffened legs defied him and he twisted and fell. Immediately the wardens were upon him. They carried him to one of the alcoves flanking the dais. Here rings had been provided to hold a man's arms in such a position that even if he fainted, his body would still remain erect. To these he was fastened, facing down the body of the church.

In the hour before the assembly arrived his consciousness slipped several times into a delirious half-sleep that was more like a lapse in time than any human condition. When he awoke, the assembly of staff and students had mainly entered and taken their places on the blocks of stone. The preceptor entered last, clad now in ceremonial dress like some majestic cleric. He spared Bron and his misery only a fleeting glance. The service was long and tedious, full of responses and intricate psalms, and the sermons were dogmatic beyond reason.

Bron, striving to combat the gulfs of blackness that interrupted his thinking, tried to gauge from the expressions of the assembly the true feelings of the individuals toward his plight. The dominant look was of interest and participation. Only a very few, like the preceptor, were twisted with the basic streak of sadism. For the rest it was part of the accepted norm.

Jaycee's voice broke in with sudden urgency. *Bron, this is what we've been waitin' for. We can hear the sound of heavy scudders movin' in. We can expect the Destroyers at any moment.*

As if to verify her words, a long explosion rumbled through the corridors and resonated in the cavity of the hall. The preceptor faltered only slightly in his prayer, then continued. A second explosion, more staccato this time, shattered the inner door.

An immediate panic was stilled as a group of armed soldiers rushed through the smoke-filled doorway. They deployed themselves professionally across the end of the church, waiting only for some act on the part of the assembly to cause them to open fire. The preceptor's words dribbled to a halt as he was faced with a reality he could not finally deny.

"Who are you? What do you want? Don't you know this is dedicated ground?" His voice echoed down the long hall, gathering timbre from the reverberations in the high, vaulted roof. It was unthinkable to him that his world should be violated.

The leading soldier spoke. "We 'ave Destroyer business 'ere. Where is one they call Ander 'altern?"

"He is here, making penance. I forbid him to speak."

"Quiet, old fool. It is I who give the orders." To emphasize the point a multiple gunblast ripped out three of the stained-glass windows. "Let 'altern come out or it will be men we split, not glass."

"I warn you—" The preceptor still had not grasped that his position was lost. "This behavior is sacrilegious. I demand that you leave."

A single shot through the head toppled the preceptor from the dais. His removal from the scene was so sudden that it was almost anticlimactic.

"Ander 'altern." Someone in the assembly at the back was being forced at weaponpoint to mark the quarry. The remaining raiders covered the assembly. Wisely, no resistance was offered. The Destroyer's firepower was, as ever, more than adequate for a massacre.

"Are you 'altern the syncretist?" The Destroyer leader stopped before Bron in the alcove, frowning at the manacles and the lymph-soaked shirt.

"The same."

"What they trying to do, kill you?"

The question was rhetorical but carried a refreshing draught of sanity. The Destroyer released the rings holding Bron's wrists and motioned him forward. Bron took one shocked step before his knees buckled under him and he pitched headlong to the dais. In delirium and with clouding consciousness he sought to raise his body and stand, but his arms, too, were now unequal to the task. He found himself helpless, looking up at the twisted mockery in the stare of the sacred relic.

"Jaycee—what the hell—is that thing called?"

It's a Terran child's playthin'. A replica of somethin' called a bear.

"Does it always have those eyes?"

No. A child must have played with it until its eye-buttons came loose. It's said to have once belonged to Prosper Haltern, founder both of the Onaris colony and of the Seminary.

"Oh God—the eternal joke—"

You're delirious, Bron. Lie quietly. I'm sending for Doc.

"Damn you, Jaycee—don't you see it? Gladly my cross I'd bear—damn—crosseyed bear—"

Stop talking, Bron. You're shoutin' aloud. You're . . .

But Bron was almost laughing as the great darkness closed down.

IV

BRON, THIS IS Doc. *Listen to me carefully. You're
on the Destroyer ship. They brought you aboard
while you were still unconscious. I gather they've
brought your temperature down and a Destroyer
medic has given you a good examination. Trouble
is he's come up with the wrong answer. He's decided to give you an injection of an
antihistamine—in fact, he's preparing it now.
Whatever happens, you mustn't have that injection.*

"You got something useful out of Ander?"

Yes. The shirt is woven of crel, an indigenous Onaria fungus spore notorious for its parasitic attachment to human flesh. The body's only defence is histamine. If that damn fool reduces your body histamine before those spor filaments have quit, they're liable to germinate into mature crel nodules underneath your skin. These are about the size of a Terran cherry and about two hundred thousand of them developing in your flesh would literally tear you apart.

"What do you advise?"

Find a way to avoid anything being done until the shirt has quit of its own accord. It's your only chance. Is the shirt still firm?

With an effort Bron propped himself up on one arm and explored. "It's coming away around the edges, Doc."

Good sign. It should peel fairly rapidly once it starts to go. Another fifteen minutes could see you clean. Can you hold the medic off that long?

"I can try."

Bron scanned the room quickly. Its sole door was fitted with a standard proximity lock keyed to operate only to the finger responses of those entitled to enter. Laboriously he climbed from bed, found his limbs unwilling to accommodate his action and collapsed in a heap on the floor. He dragged himself to an instrument stanchion and looked for tools with which to attack the lock. The only thing relevant was a surgical laser. Unsteadily he took it to the door.

The lock pattern was unfamiliar to him and he had no way of locating the critical sensory elements. A very real chance existed that interference would immobilize it in the open rather than the closed position. Finally he settled for merely shorting out the input leads. With a bit of luck the lock's malfunctioning would appear to have been an inherent fault and not the result of tampering. He carefully fired the laser into the input channel. The laser hole was almost invisible but the result was an untidy short-circuit that seared the finish on the door around the lock. Fortunately the damage looked sufficiently amateurish to let him remain in character.

Doc, who had been following the exercise through Bron's eyes, was critical.

How long will that hold them?

"Depends on how anxious they are to get in. Dismantling the lock would take about twenty minutes, but the door could be cut away in seconds if necessary."

Bron lurched painfully back to bed and began working his fingers cautiously between his arm and the shirt. He soon found that the shirt was losing its consistency and shredding away in the manner of cotton wool. The underlying skin was red, swollen and moist with lymph, but otherwise undamaged. As he worked at it, the fibers began to come away more easily and almost half the garment had been removed before he heard noises at the door.

The first sounds were those of someone baffled by an inability to operate the lock. Soon came the sound of metal applied to the door as if to force it. Then silence for a period. Then action again and the lock was cut away with a heavy-duty laser beam.

As the medic entered, Bron, propped on one arm, was engaged in removing the last fragments of the shirt from his breast. As far as he could judge, the filaments adhering to his back had largely rubbed away on the bedding. The medic examined the lock with some consternation, at the same time glancing across to Bron and the fragmented shirt. Since there was no obvious connection between these two things, he left the lock to a technician and came across the room

"You got it away, eh? How you manage tha'?"

"It's histamine sensitive." The swelling in Bron's throat had raised the pitch of his voice to a querulous piping tone. He lay back with a show of exhaustion he did not have to fake.

"Why you do it, eh? Why you put tha' damn thing on?"

Bron searched the synthesis but found no answer, so he scowled and said, "The shirt is an accepted penance in the eyes of the church."

"Bloody funny church—damn masochis's, all of them. Are there no psychiatris's on Onaris?"

"Certainly. I myself have a doctorate in psychiatry," said Bron Ander Haltern tiredly. "But what makes you think that ills of the spirit are curable by techniques designed to remedy mere malfunctions of the mind?"

The medic refused to be drawn into what he regarded as an idiotic argument. "Turn over and let me see tha' back."

Bron turned. The medic cleaned his back with spirit and wiped away the remaining fibers of the shirt, retaining some for closer examination. He found the crucifix around Bron's neck, looked at it curiously, dropped it back.

"I'm goin' to give you injection. With luck your skin should clear in a few hours. You'll find the side effec's of the drug will make you li'le silly."

"Accept or refuse, Doc?"

Risk the injection now that the fibers have quit—but if you get a swelling yell like a fiend until they cut it out.

The medic turned to get his tray. As he did so Bron could see past him to the doorway. Standing just inside, a silent witness to the proceedings, was a tall, graying man of exceptional physique and bearing. He was clad immaculately in the uniform of a senior Destroyer officer, though his precise rank was not apparent. His attention was completely upon Bron, with a depth of concentration and comprehension that made Bron feel that the hypno-synthesis was a very shallow camouflage for concealing his true identity and purpose.

"Who's that?" asked Bron aloud as the medic returned.

"Colonel Daiquis'." Both the medic and Doc replied as nearly simultaneously as possible, but Doc Veeder's identification carried undertones of awe.

What a piece of luck, Bron. Martin Daiquist is Cana's right-hand man.

Bron withdrew his arm from the vicinity of the hypodermic gun. "I wish to see someone in authority. I was brought here without consent and I have no wish to remain. I demand to be returned to the Seminary.''

The medic looked down pityingly. ''Tomorrow someone will explain why tha's impossible.'' His fingers gripped Bron's arm like a steel vise. ''From now until then you do exactly as you're tol'.''

Past the medic's shoulder Bron could see Colonel Daiquist examining the door around the lock. Then he saw him straighten suddenly and look round as if searching for something. The hypodermic gun was back on Bron's arm, the muzzle pressing hard as the molecularized drugs were introduced through his skin without puncture. Almost immediately Bron felt a heavy dreamlike state come over him, bringing a touch of euphoria that left him quite without care or qualm as Daiquist picked up the surgical laser and took it to the door.

Perhaps on the altar of some Satanic mass the screaming sacrifice, shackled to the stone, twists in torment. The descending dagger tears tendon and ligament but leaves alive the cowering consciousness . . .

''Who's that?''

. . .WHY DO YOU KEEP ON PRAYING? DON'T YOU KNOW THAT GOD IS DEAD?

''Tell me who you are or I'll go to sleep on you.''

Don't do that, Bron. I'm having a hard enough task getting through to you as it is. I'm Ananias.

''Go away. I don't know you.''

Don't you remember me at all? Don't you even

recall that Ananias is a liar?

"Ananias is merely a name. I can't remember a thing. You must be the joker of the pack."

Frequently, Bron. But right now I'm far from joking. What drugs did the medic give you?

"Should have been antihistamine and antiallergen."

But you didn't see the labels on the phials?

"No. He preloaded the hypodermic. I want to go to sleep."

Not so fast. From your poor reaction to the semantic recall I'd say the medic included a measure of a hypnotic alkaloid, possibly a truth serum.

"Damn you, let me sleep!"

I will—soon. But while you're sleeping I think someone may attempt to question you. Daiquist's not too happy about you for some reason. We can't rely on the synthesis holding out under intensive psychological probing. If the situation turns critical we intend to use one of our corrective circuits to throw you into a state of catatonic withdrawal. They'll soon get you out of it, but it should serve to confuse the situation.

The effort of conversation had pulled Bron into a lighter level of sleep from which he now found himself unable to relax. He tried to open his eyes, but the effort nearly defeated him and he was unable to maintain them open. In any case, the room was completely dark and there was nothing whatever to see. His mind settled down to a level of activity characteristic of a dream state but which left him fully conscious. This limbo of thought between sleep and waking was positive confirmation of the introduction of a hypnotic drug into his system.

He likened his feeling to those of a man floating on an air raft borne over slow waters down a long tunnel of darkness. The almost complete absence of tactile sensation, coupled with the free-flowing volume of his thoughts and heightened imagination, produced all the imagery necessary to give substance to the illusion. He even thought he could hear the echoed muttering of the tide, disturbed by his passage, lapping against tunnel walls . . .

Shock! Even in his drugged condition his whole nervous system reacted fitfully.

"Ananias, for God's sake—"

What is it, Bron?

"What's that noise? Sounds like turkeys gobbling—or water rippling around a stone."

I hear nothing but ship noises. Sure it's not imagination?

"Damn you, no. It must be coming over the bio-electronic transfer link."

Not possible. We're transmitting nothing but my voice. The computer's monitoring the output from the Antares transmitter to you and that doesn't show any variation except for the usual star static.

"Well, I'm receiving something else and it's unholy—like the sound of liquid geese. Is it possible for anything else to get impressed on your transmission—something you couldn't detect?"

Only if it came from a source below the Antares reception threshold. But there's nowhere it could come from. There's only the void on the other side of your present position. You're way out on the rim of the universe.

"Can they increase the sensitivity of the Antares receivers?"

Not without rebuilding half a planet. Can you still hear it?

"It's still there, but not so clearly. The ambient ship noise seems to be increasing."

Correct. Sounds as though they're preparing for lift-off. I doubt you'll get any visitors until the ship's in free space. If you want to sleep, this'll be a good time.

"Ananias—"

Yes?

"Did we ever meet, you and I?"

We know each other rather well. One day you'll remember.

"And Jaycee—I know her?"

I can't answer questions about Jaycee. That's classified.

"I just wondered what I ever did to get paired up with a vindictive bitch like her."

Bron attempted to relax, to throw himself into less conscious depths of slumber, but each time his mind washed up on the same dark, tunneled tide and stopped short at the same reactive fear. The sound of the rising pattern of activity in the ship gradually overlaid the phantom goose-mutter from nowhere and drove it below the limits of discernibility. The rising crescendo of the pressor beam projectors began to vibrate the whole fabric of the ship and the beats of their misresonance sang like some awful electronic choir.

Then he felt the lift-off—only a few meters at first, while the pressors were trimmed to take the weight of the ship evenly and without straining the vast structure. The breath-taking thunder of the planetary drive boomed in above the pressors' song and added a quarter gravity of horizontal component of movement to the pressor's lift. Some loose instruments somewhere in the room clattered into a tray, otherwise inside the ship these maneuvers were deceptively smooth and gentle. Outside the ship it would be different. Bron winced at the thought of white-hot exhaust gas razing a kilometer-wide weal across the scarred face of Ashur and of pressors leaving a hundred-kilometer channel of pulverized buildings and hopelessly compressed soil before the ship abandoned planetary support and began to claw its way through the troposphere by thrust reaction alone.

As the successive phases of takeoff approached, the pitch and timbre of the engine voices altered, died, were replaced by other sounds. Soon even the scream of the atmosphere on the hull tailed away and the ship settled to the vibrant thunder of the main gravity drive, which would be its prime mover until it was clear of the planetary system of which Onaris was part. Not until then could the cumbersome physical drive systems be abandoned in favor of the delicate subspace mechanisms which could flip the ship to its destination at megalight velocities without regard to mass or momentum.

Slowly Bron's ears became attuned to the dissonance of the engine, and he even dived into fitful sleep before becoming aware that the light in the room had been turned on and that two men had arrived at his side.

"Ander Haltern." This was a statement, not an address.

"Ah, so that's our master syncretist. He looks too young. You know, Martin, they say he's one of the most brilliant men alive."

"He came in wearing a shirt of some parasitic fungus. If that's brilliance, I prefer mediocrity." The second voice held a crisp bitterness of tone. A hand reached down and pulled at the crucifix on the chain, then let it to again.

"Chacun à son gout—sorry, Martin, I forgot you hated the old world and its babels. But every man to his own choice. Not everyone has a hobby such as yours—or is in a position to indulge in it even if he so desired."

"You've never objected before." The phrase was swiftly defensive.

"My dear Martin, I am not objecting. I was merely making the point that his desire to suffer pain and your desire to inflict it are merely two aspects of the same sort of character distortion."

A long, irritated silence fell.

Then: "Do you want to question him?"

"I don't particularly want a recital of hick-world lineage and aspirations tonight, Martin. We know he's Haltern, or he wouldn't have been where he was when we found him. Whether he's a prime catalyst we shan't know until we get to the rendezvous."

You listening, Bron?

"Yes." Subvocally.

Can you open your eyes and look at them. We've got the cameras on. A short blink will do.

Bron shifted his head as though in disturbed sleep, then fought his eyelids open for a few bleared instants while he focused on the faces of the two men beside him.

Nicely done, Bron. We've got what we wanted. One's Martin Daiquist, whom you've already seen. The other—man, you certainly pick your company well!

"Spool it, Ananias! I'm not thinking well to-night."

Just as well, perhaps. You've just been face to face with Cana himself.

V

HE AWOKE TO the sound of a watch bell and sat up, shaking the sleep from his head. As the medic had predicted, his skin had cleared, except for a slight scale which feathered away as he touched it. The ache in his limbs, too, was now scarcely perceptible.

"Anyone awake?" He addressed his unseen mentors in a spirit of bravado.

Awake? Jaycee was annoyed. *How the hell can anyone be otherwise with you snorin' your head off over the transfer link? How do you feel?*

"Like it was Christmas in Europa."

Good. Your memory's returnin'. Though with your usual intake of drink and drugs it beats me how you ever managed to recall anythin' of Christmas in Europa.

"Tell me about Daiquist. I'm sure he suspected I fixed that door."

Martin Daiquist, ninth generation, Cana's lieutenant—and probably more ruthless than Cana himself. Responsible for the punitive expeditions against the four worlds that held out against the formation of the Destroyer federation. Watch out for him. He's a mean cuss and as perceptive as the devil. His hobby is takin' people apart painfully.

"I'll bear that in mind. What are he and Cana doing here?"

We're still not sure. Neither would normally concern himself with a mere planetary raid. Either there's somethin' big online or else they've sensed the Commando interest in the raid and come to investigate personally. If the latter is the case, don't try any of your usual fool—

She broke off to give Bron a chance to concentrate as the medic entered. He gave Bron a swift but thorough examination.

"You bloody clear," he said. "You don' deserve it, treatin' your skin like tha'. I'll get you breakfas' sent, an' then you clear out, eh? An' if you come back here again, nex' time I'll use the knife on you—without anaesthetics. See how much masochis' you are. Colonel Daiquis' wants to see you—an' I don' advise you play the fool with him. I can' patch up a body after he's done.''

Soon an orderly fetched a hot breakfast on a tray and the smell of baked meats and coffee made Bron wonder when he had last eaten. He could not remember. His own activities prior to the raid were still lost to him. The orderly also delivered a packet of clothing. Bron found inside a light-weight, tunic-style uniform, underclothes and a white gown that was presumably used for bathing and relaxation. Compressing his lips in wry amusement, he selected only the underclothes and the gown. Fortunately the gown had a pocket large enough to accommodate the Bible. The remaining garments he dropped into the surgical disposal chute, an action he felt certain was in keeping with his position as a Haltern.

When the medic came to escort him to Daiquist he raised his eyebrows at Bron's choice of apparel. ''You're bloody mad you don' do as you're tol'.'' But his acceptance of Bron's assumed eccentricity was an encouraging sign that the incredible masquerade was viable and working.

Daiquist looked up from his desk as Bron entered.

''Ah, the syncretist. You seem to have recovered.''

''Why am I here?'' asked Bron sharply. ''I demand to be returned to the Seminary.''

Daiquist cocked his head on one side. ''There's

59

no chance of that—no chance at all. Even if we wished, it wouldn't be possible. And we don't wish. We came a long way to get you, Haltern."

"The familiar is Bron," said Bron archly.

"Very well—Bron. But don't mistake your position. You are a prisoner just as surely as if you were chained to a wall. We hope—ultimately—to gain your cooperation. Until we do—and have satisfied ourselves of your integrity—you must consider yourself under close guard. I had myself preferred you to be conveyed in the fleshholds, but I was overruled. However, you will end up there if you engage in any mischief.

Shortly the door opened and Cana himself came into the room. He looked searchingly at Bron, then took Daiquist's place behind the desk. The impression he gave was that of a powerful intellectual rather than a ruthless creator and destroyer of empires.

"Leave us, will you, Martin."

For a moment Daiquist appeared about to protest, then he turned and left the room, with a meaningful glance at the prisoner. Bron sensed that a dissension had already arisen over his status on the ship. Daiquist was profoundly displeased.

Alone with the great space tyrant, Bron sensed the magnitude of the man—Cana seemed to fill the room with a hypnotic presence.

"I don't normally intervene in Martin's affairs," said Cana. "But I can't afford to have a syncretist of your standing exposed to Martin's personal curiosity. By all accounts you're a man of many talents. You could be very useful to us. But Martin's a suspicious devil—a quality that often makes him invaluable. He has a theory about you, Syncretist. He suspects you are not who you claim to be."

"I'm Bron Ander Haltern, master syncretist, late of Adano University on Onaris."

"If that's so, then you won't mind answering a few questions. If you get a word wrong I'll leave you to Martin."

"I object to my word's being doubted. I'll answer anything you care to ask." The synthesis was responding weakly but he picked up the feeling and amplified it himself, exaggerating the note of aggrievement.

Bron, this could be sticky. I'm getting Ander on the line to back you up.

"Check, Jaycee. I'm not getting much from the synthesis."

Cana went to a cabinet and drew out a sheaf of papers. "You see, Bron Haltern, we already know quite a lot about you. Where is Jeddah?"

Trick question. Jeddah's a town on Onaris—but the one a Haltern would remember first is Jeddah Haltern. He's dead.

The voice in Bron's head was unfamiliar, but had a strong Onaris accent.

"Jeddah's dead," said Bron. The synthesis stirred weakly. "He was fifth generation. Had he lived he'd have been a hundred and seven by now."

Good, but don't take chances.

Cana nodded and leafed through the sheets until he came to some plainly tabulated lists.

"Give me the title of the paper you presented to the Ninth Symposium of Galactic Science at Maroc on Priam."

The ninth symposium was on Mela five, not Priam. Priam was the tenth.

"Which do you want," asked Bron, "the paper from the tenth conference or the one given on Mela five?"

"Mela five, of course," said Cana, without looking back at the sheets. "I must have mistaken the line."

The Application of the Advancing-parameter Exclusion Theory to the Prognostic Delineation of the Patterns of Chaos.

Bron repeated this verbatim. Cana nodded and threw the sheaf of papers back on the table.

"You know, Syncretist, I don't entirely disagree with Martin. He has an instinct for these things and he's seldom wrong. He daren't be wrong. Our survival is often entirely in his hands. So I reserve an open mind. But if you aren't Haltern, then whoever did send you schooled you well—so well, perhaps, that whether you are the original or an impostor could be largely irrelevant."

"Now answer me a question," said Bron, watching the man closely. "Why have the Destroyer nations such urgent need for a master syncretist?"

"Not just a master syncretist. They come in all calibers, and we already have most of them. What we most needed was a man who could combine syncretics with an appreciation of the patterns of chaos."

"Why?"

"In a few hours," said Cana, "we are making a space rendezvous. When we are clear from there I may answer your question—or I may not. You may even answer it for yourself. Until then you have the freedom of the ship. The armorer will take your fingering for the proxlocks. You may enter any doors that open to you. The others are permanently barred to you. I'll have the quartermaster find you cabin-space."

Cana stood up, waved at the door. Bron needed no second indication of dismissal. He made his way straight to the den of the armorer. The latter took his fingering for the proxlocks and entered the resulting profiles in the access computer.

Bron made an experimental tour of most of the open levels of the ship to verify his freedom of the locks. Incredibly, almost all the doors he tried responded to his touch. Back in the small cabin which had been allocated to him, he lay back on the bunk and called up his unseen confederates.

"Jaycee?"

No. This is Ananias. Honey-bitch is feeding—I suspect on her usual diet of ground-glass and snake venom. What do you make of Cana's giving you the freedom of the ship?

"I'm not quite sure. The main question is why. I suspect I'm being allowed just about enough rope to hang from, unless I've got it calculated wrong. The only sectors I haven't been able to enter are Weaponry, Communications and part of the computing complex. It's too damn easy. I'm willing to bet they log every meter I move."

How about the control room? We need to know the ship's destination as soon as possible.

"I've not yet tried Control. I don't dare seem too interested in the machinery here. Anyway, there's some sort of space rendezvous coming up shortly and the chances are that our heading will be different from there out. Once they start setting for a subspace hop I can pick up the coordinates straight from the subspace matrices if necessary—without even entering control."

Good idea. Mind you, they shouldn't be too worried. If they keep you out of Communications they can be reasonably confident that whatever you learn can't be relayed to where it might be dangerous. I think our concept of the bio-electronic transfer link is sufficiently unique for it to remain completely unsuspected.

"I wish I were sure it is unique. I'm still worried about that goose-gobble I heard. Something else is operating on our transmission band. It certainly wasn't star static or a normal sort of interference."

From calculation it seems that there's nothing near you in space that could conceivably be the signal source. The present hypothesis is that it's a heterodyne signal from something on the ship itself.

"It was no heterodyne. I'd say it had all the elements of an intelligent semantic content based on an advanced-level communications system."

I'll follow it up, but I think you're certainly wrong. Hullo! What are they doing with your engines?

Bron listened critically. "Applying retro, I

think. Could mean we're approaching rendezvous.''

Rendezvous with what?

''It hasn't been said or implied, but I'd guess
with the remainder of the Destroyer fleet, including those that held orbit round Onaris during the
raid.''

*I wonder why. They wouldn't dare to attempt to
hold formation in subspace, so why assemble be-
forehand?*

''Sounds as though they're putting call signs on
the boards right now. The center of attention
seems to be the chartroom.''

*Better not look too nosy. Wait till the rendezvous
has been established, then go up.*

''Are you giving me orders, Ananias?''

Yes. Have you forgotten how to take them?

''Let's get this straight,'' said Bron. ''I'm on the
operating end of the transfer link. Mine's the hide
that pays for any mistakes and mine's the body
they consign to space when the charade goes sour.
Ask for any information you need, but how and
when I obtain it is my option. If you want a puppet,
jet off and buy yourself a doll.''

Say that softly, little soldier. Anania's voice was
dangerous. *You've more than one electrode in your
brain and the controls are under my fingers on this
console. Shall I read the decals? Catatonic Withdrawal. Anaesthesia With Maintained Consciousness. Punishment. Death. They aren't written that way, of course—we're great believers in
the use of symbols to gloss over the earthier and
more painful facts of your existence—but the ef-*

fects are just those. You see, we can insist on discipline.

"You've forgotten a button, Ananias."

I think not.

"While you're playing at being God, shouldn't you also have one with the symbol for resurrection?"

The sudden cutoff of the gravity drive threw a vast silence over Bron's immediate environs, a stillness punctuated only by muted ship noises. The call boards were still chiming the reassembly call. Bron left his cabin and went to investigate. For several minutes the gangways were full of crewmen hastening to regroup. Moving aside to allow one to pass, Bron was instead saluted smartly.

"Mastership Haltern, Cana wishes you to join Colonel Daiquist and himself in the chartroom."

Bron nodded, trying to analyze the attitude of the crewman. His instructions appeared to include the implication to treat Bron with the respect due a Destroyer officer. This could only be a reflection of Haltern's value as a master syncretist to the Destroyer nations. A suspicion slowly formed.

"Ananias, answer me something. What factors made you so sure Ander Haltern was the only man on Onaris the Destroyers would select?"

A knowledge of the Onaris intellectual scene coupled with some good guesswork. Why?

"Because the fact that it worked is too damn much of a coincidence. They must have had a very distinct reason for picking up Haltern alone and you must have known exactly what that reason was. Now give me the facts.''

I already have given them to you.

"Liar."

Ananias laughed softly. *So you do remember just a little about Ananias?*

"Only that you aren't to be trusted."

Of course not. But there's absolutely nothing you can do about it.

"Think again, Ananias," said Bron. "As agent on this team I've a right to any information I consider relevant. Tell Doc I want a straight answer to the question I asked you—the data so far available looks very suspect."

In the chartroom he found the atmosphere electric with tension. All the navigation staff, including those off duty, were gathered to watch the screens. In the deep-space sector station both Daiquist and Cana were present, watching points of light against the cosmic black.

Daiquist looked up, saw Bron and scowled, then beckoned him to join them. By the time Bron had reached the deep-sector station all eyes were again intent on the screens and no explanations were offered. Daiquist was supervising some chronometric plotting—whatever event was about to take place obviously had time as an important component of the equation. Bron settled for a position with a good view of a subsidiary monitoring screen, a situation which also afforded him an opportunity to watch the activities in the whole station. The screen itself gave him an impressive view of the bright ring of ships of the Destroyer fleet now locked in tight formation and motionless, waiting for something to happen.

As the minutes passed, so the tension grew. Then, as if following some indefinable clue, the deep-space controller signaled.

"I think this is it."

He rapidly centered some almost invisible object under the graticules of his screen and began calling coordinates. All the other scanners turned outward to face the depths of space, though few others had the range to detect an object at such a distance. Daiquist and Cana pressed forward to look over the controller's shoulder. The displayed image as yet had no form, being a mere scatter of electronic noise.

Within seconds the computers had acquired sufficient data to begin processing and the screen picture steadied to a rocklike concentricity in the graticules as electronic fingers searched and corrected for the minute signal reflection from some remote splint of matter far in the emptiness of space.

"That's it."

Cana had acquired a printout from a computer peripheral and a second printout terminal was already making a comparison with something set deep in the computer's micro-memory cells.

Daiquist returned to the chronometric plotting and watched the pantograph arms begin to sweep wide curves across the plotting boards. His lips grew taut.

"Only sixteen point one hours late this time. The positional accuracy is exact and the chronological accuracy is still improving."

"Damn," said Cana. "Still I suppose we must be thankful for those two certainties among all the patterns of chaos. I'm getting a bit old for entropy." He glanced up and saw Bron's quizzical interest. For a second his eyes looked into Bron's with a depth of comprehension that rocked Bron back on his heels.

"I have a curious feeling about you, Syncretist. There's something in your face that suggests you know what chaos is. I just wonder if your being here is a fact any less calculated than the timing and trajectory of *those*."

He nodded back to the screens. Bron's eyes followed, fascinated, as the range closed and the scanners steadily improved in resolution, tumbling slowly and aimlessly through the depths of space. The speed with which the details improved was a measure of the very considerable velocity with which the object was moving, yet viewed through the screens against the backdrop of the farther galaxies, its progress appeared leisurely indeed.

As it neared it became more distinct in form. Seven long, thick, black cylinders, reminiscent of those used for compressed gas, had been strapped to a thick, black yoke. That appeared to be all; no instruments, no antenna, no solar panels were visible—none of the delicate and complex sensory and corrective mechanisms usually associated with unmanned space-traversing objects. If anything, the overall impression was one of extreme age and durability rather than of technological prowess. There was something incredibly sinister about these black canisters tumbling idly through space.

The scanners were now producing almost a close-up view of the object and the hideous weld seams, massive and unfettled, stood out plainly. Had somebody broken off a part of some ancient gas-cooking plant and hurled it carelessly into space, the effect would have been similar. But there was nothing careless about its trajectory, to judge from the meticulous care with which its path was being recorded by the Destroyer technicians. Some great and desperate event seemed about to happen, but everyone about Bron was too intent on some given task to offer explanations.

He gasped as the reeling mass filled the screens, as though falling straight upon Cana's ship. But this was a trick of screen magnification. Suddenly the scanners reeled and Bron found himself watching the object falling away in a higgledy-piggledy tumble as it passed through the ring of watching ships.

Daiquist was again busy watching the chronometric plotting, as successive sweeps of the pantograph thickened the once faint traces to multiple bands of lines like the diagram of a muscular skeleton. Cana watched the cylinders draw away, his face a cloud of darkness. Then with sudden decision he turned his back on the screens and walked away.

His path took him past Bron and his eyes widened sagely.

"Watch that one through, Syncretist. I shall want to talk to you after."

Wondering, Bron stepped forward into Cana's vacated seat with the main screen in full view before him. Remorselessly the crossed hairs of the screen graticule locked on to the path of the retreating canisters, which appeared to diminish slowly in size and then advance again as the magnification was periodically adjusted to offset the increasing range. Bron followed their dark passage with deep interest. The nemesis appeared to have passed, but the tension in the chartroom was undiminished. So intent was he on following the progress of the cylinders framed at the center of the screen that he neglected the implication of the changing hues of the background.

Onaris! Ananias's voice broke in on his thoughts. *Give us a broader view, Bron.*

Bron scanned the whole screen area, realizing with a start that the variegated background hues were, in reality, the non-focused outlines of seas and continents. Inexorably the black cylinders continued under the crossed hairs of the graticule, while the physical details of the planetary surface began to grow in resolution.

The moment of impact was unforgettable.

The blossoming fireball must have extended into space a full planetary diameter, a gulf of fantastic fiery plasma that streaked up and out with a velocity beyond the regions of belief. From his knowledge of physics Bron knew that such a fantastic holocaust must have stripped the atmosphere from the planet in seconds. The next stage was a sort of coalescence, the fireball contracting and drawing in upon itself as if to concentrate its essence. The color shifted from red to brilliant yellow, surrealistic with an ethereal fringe of mercurial blue. Around it the planetary features reappeared, but not with the cool greens and buffs of before. Now whole continents stood out as if raised to cherry heat, and where the seas had been were bowls of black, crawling with fire like soot on a chimney.

Then the planet broke up, not quickly, but with the wrong-seeming slowness of massive events seen from a distance; a kind of reluctant finality. Centered upon the spot where the fireball had condensed, the planet began to spew up its liquid core in a gout of molten heavy metals, which coalesced in space and drew back toward the gravitic center of the mass, obliterating continents and coastlines with a horrific tide of matter returned to the state from which the planet had once cooled. As this happened, the shell of the planet broke, continents rearing crazily on end like ships sinking on a sea and land masses floating in broken fragments like dross on molten tin.

Bron kept no record of the hours that passed while this incredible scene was enacted. The death of individuals was something he had been trained to accept unconditionally; the death of nations was one of the aims of war. Even whole species died occasionally in the name of some cause—but the death of an entire planet was something that rendered Man and his entire status in the universe of no greater account than a biological culture grown in a dish and discarded when the experiment was finished. This was an object lesson in finite reality.

VI

"ALL RIGHT, ANANIAS, so I've seen it. Now explain it to me." Bron's voice was hardened by his viewing of the incident.

How do you think they got the name Destroyers, Bron?

"But where did the hellburner come from? It didn't originate from this fleet."

It wouldn't. A ship carrying weapons like that would scarcely be invited to make planetfall on a flesh raid. Even in standoff orbit it could be a liability. They must keep it clear out in the void. When the raid is finished it slides in a massive hellburner to take care of the evidence.

"I shouldn't have thought that Cana needed to destroy the evidence. He's strong enough not to care what the Galaxy thinks."

In five years galactic patrols have found around thirty-seven formerly inhabited planets turned into nickel-iron slag balls. Eleven of these, equipped with subspace transmitters, had broadcast warnings of Destroyer attack shortly before their obliteration. Five others put out standard light-velocity-limited transmissions with the same theme. Some of these planets were dead three years before anyone got the message.

Bron considered this in silence for a moment.

"Tell me, Ananias, what was the population of Onaris?"

About two hundred million.

"Then if we knew the Destroyers were coming when they did, why the hell didn't we have a fleet waiting for them instead of only me?"

If we'd known that Daiquist and Cana were with the party, we probably would have had our fleet there. As it was we were merely implementing a policy decision to locate their baseworld.

"Policy decision? That decision just cost two hundred million Onarians their lives. What kind of policy is that?"

Bron froze as a hand clamped on his shoulder. Daiquist dropped into the seat next to him.

"Why so thoughtful, Syncretist? Have you never seen a world destroyed before?"

"That was Onaris," said Bron flatly. "All gone. In the name of God, why did you have to do it?

You'd presumably already taken all that you came for."

Daiquist's eyes were searching Bron's face critically. "I rather wonder if we didn't get a little more than we came for. You make me uneasy, Syncretist. I never did have much time for intellectuals—and an intellectual with the build and tone of a fighting man definitely needs watching. For myself I wouldn't take the risk. I'd prefer to kill you now, but Cana has decided otherwise. I advise you to prove him right."

Bron returned the scrutiny in depth. "You still haven't answered my question. Why was it necessary to destroy Onaris?"

"Syncretist you may be," said Daiquist, "but you've still got a hell of a lot to learn. Come, Cana wants to see you in his suite. We're going to give you the chance to do a little exercise in cooperation."

"Cooperation? My God—you expect me to cooperate with you after *that*?" He made a dramatic gesture toward the spotted fire-cherry that was all that was left of Onaris on the screen. "I would rather die."

"I'd rather you died," said Daiquist. "Unfortunately the decision isn't mine. But listen carefully to what Cana has to say, because it's likely you'll change your mind."

"You don't bend a Haltern that easily. Damn you, Daiquist! If I must take this journey, let it be in the flesh holds." The synthesis still stirred weakly.

Steady, Bron. Ananias's voice was cautioning.

"I don't happen to be offering you the choice." Daiquist drew his sidearm menacingly. "It's not a good idea to keep Cana waiting. If you're thinking of resistance—remember that I never shoot to kill."

Having no option, Bron rose and reluctantly walked in the indicated direction. Daiquist followed, his weapon aimed low. At the door of Cana's suite Bron was surprised to find the lock respond easily to his own hand. Cana was sitting at a large desk, watching strip issuing from a computer printout terminal. This had evidently been his occupation for some time, for the floor was littered with discarded strip lengths printed with compact series of figures.

"Ah, Syncretist." Cana kicked the sprawling strips into an untidy pile. "Stay with us, will you, Martin."

"It might be wisest." Daiquist selected a chair and gestured Bron to another. Cana addressed himself to Bron.

"I take it from your face that you've seen what happened to Onaris."

"I've seen what happened. What I can't establish is why it was necessary. Surely you'd already taken what you wanted?"

Cana frowned, a display indicating a depth of concentration outside Bron's experience.

"You won't understand this yet, but it was precisely because we'd taken what we wanted that Onaris died. Almost our only means of establishing the success of a raid is whether a hellburner blasts the life out of the target planet within hours of our liftoff.''

Bron was silent for a long second, wrestling with the wrongness of this statement. Finally he looked back at Cana and shook his head.

"That doesn't make sense."

"It does to us. The point I wish to make clear to you is that we didn't put that hellburner down there. Somebody else did."

He's lying, Bron. Ananias's voice was positive.

"You don't expect me to believe that?"

"In the circumstances, no. I know your intellectual record and I realize it precludes you from accepting a statement unless you are satisfied with the evidence on which it's based. I'm therefore giving you the opportunity of establishing and examining your own evidence—and drawing your own conclusions."

"How?"

"I invite—no, dare you—to examine any available record from any ship of this fleet and attempt to calculate the source and time of origin of the missile that destroyed Onaris. Two points I would add. One—although the missile's position was exact, its arrival was sixteen point one hours late in time. Two—" Cana swung full-face to Bron for emphasis and Daiquist raised his sidearm meaningly—"you may have access to our video records of the screens and any other data in our possession to enable you to calculate the missile's exact point of impact on Onaris. Although its effect would have been the same wherever it had struck, I think you'll find its point of impact coincides exactly with your own position sixteen point one hours earlier. You see, Bron Haltern, that missile wasn't specifically intended for Onaris— or even for us. That missile was intended for you—personally.''

What you makin' of it, Bron?
"Not sure, Jaycee. Could be an elaborate sort of game—a trick to secure the cooperation of whatever intelligentsia they have lifted in a raid. Or it could be that Cana's quite genuine when he says that the Destroyers aren't to blame.''

Ananias doesn't think so. He was as mad as a scalded tiger when you accepted Cana's invitation to check out the data on the hellburner.

"I'm not sure that I trust Ananias any more than I trust Cana. Do you record everything that transpires over the transfer link?''

It's all sound- and video-taped for future reference. Why?

"Tell Doc I'd like to check back through the sessions I've had with Ananias. I'm not convinced I'm getting the right answers.''

Uh! Even in amnesia the mistrust isn't dead. If you're takin' on Ananias you'd best be reminded he's a pretty dangerous cuss.

"So am I, Jaycee. And the way I see this mission, it's strictly one-way, so I don't have anything to lose. Will you do it?''

With pleasure. I'd love to get hold of somethin'

that would make the Godlost weaklin' sweat.

"Then stay on the line—because there are things about General Ananias that I'm beginning to remember."

Bron had acquired a master-program panel in part of the computing complex to which he had access. Two Destroyer programers had been assigned to him and a duty technician was on sound and vision call. All were quickly supplying whatever services or data Bron chose to ask for. Bron, relying less on the failing Haltern synthesis than on his own training, was speedily assessing his requirements and impressing the information on a standard location-of-source space-weapons program. The information available from the ring of Cana's fleetships through which the object had passed added a dimensional certainty to his calculation that was normally lacking in similar studies.

Cana can't hope to get away with this, Bron. Any computerman worth his salt and given access to the data you're gettin' must be able to give the lie to the claim.

"Unless the computer is bent. There's a lot of this computing complex I can't get near. They could be using it to apply correctives so that I can only get the answers they want me to have."

That's why we're readin' everythin' through you, Bron. We're going to run the same computation here so we can compare differences.

"Fine. I'm just about through on the location-of-source program. I'll set it running."

We're going to rewrite the program to suit our

equipment. We've got all the data we need, so we won't be far behind you.

Bron called the Destroyer technician. "How's that video record coming on?"

"She nearly ready, if you like to come up to projection room."

Bron cast a hurried glance over his own series of figures, then passed it to the programers. In the projection room the technician was waiting.

"Ah've put the las' two hundred frames before explosion on closed loop. Give you las' four seconds of approach withou' spoilin' definition."

"Run it."

Bron dropped into a seat before the screens.

The Destroyer technician looked at him briefly; his smile acknowledged the professional competence in Bron's way of organizing his inquiries. "Ah'll put her on big screen, Mr. 'altern."

"The form of address is Mastership," said Bron severely. "Have you got that reconnaissance photograph of Ashur yet?"

"Jus' comin' on facsimile printer. Soon as scan is complete we'll print projection slide for montage."

"I don't want montage. I want to alternate the scanner image with the reconnaissance projection."

"Ah get poin' now. You alternate two images a' same magnification, you able pinpoin' position of contac' within few hundred meters."

"To be certain, I need to locate to within one meter."

The technician whistled. "Tha's no' possible, Mastership."

"Call me Bron."

The technician smiled broadly. "Ah'm Camaj. You no amateur, Bron. You know wha' you're doin'. Ah've tried some fixes in my time, but this the closes' Ah ever tried."

"Can you do it?"

"A fix to one meter from t'irty million kilometers? You need be jokin'."

"I'm not joking, Camaj. I do need that accuracy to be sure."

"Then we do i' as you say. You show me how."

The screen lit up with the video-recorded last four seconds before the missile struck, repeated endlessly from the closed tape loop. In these last fragments of time for Onaris, the image of the city of Ashur flashed briefly into focus, a mere vague pattern of blocked browns and grays, unrecognizable as it stood, meaningful only if compared with a more detailed view. Central in the field of view was the black shape of the missile still aimlessly atwist in the instants before its terrible reaction.

The scene was swiftly replaced with a projected reconnaissance holograph of Ashur taken from a ship orbiting around Onaris before the cataclysm. Here the ground details stood out with perfect clarity, with buildings, vehicles, and even the minute dots of individuals easily identifiable. The magnification of the projection was adjusted to that of the taped record and then the two images were alternated to show coincidences of outline.

Roughly half the reconnaissance record had been traversed before the two patterns showed point for point similarity. Bron's final micro-adjustments took fully half an hour.

"Jaycee, what was my exact position sixteen point one hours before the explosion?"

You were chained in the alcove at the west end of the church of the Sacred Relic. The Destroyer party was just about to collect you.

"You saw where the hellburner struck?"

Yes. At the west end of the church slightly to the right of the centerline. In other words, it went as near as possible right down on to that alcove.

"Correct. Which is too much of a coincidence to be true. I don't like coincidences that can be measured with a micrometer attachment."

He glanced up and saw the technician watching him. "Convinced, Camaj?"

"Ah'm convinced. Tha' technique Ah use again. Will tha' be enough?"

Bron nodded. "More than enough to be going on with. How the hell does anyone project a hellburner from out-space with that sort of accuracy?"

The technician shrugged his shoulders. "You're th' syncretis'. For me, wonder is how she gets through atmosphere withou' burnou'. After all, she has no nose cone—"

"Jaycee, you heard that?"

Yes, Bron. We'd picked up the same point. Not only remarkable weaponry, but a remarkable weapon too. It should have burned out in the at-

mosphere at that velocity, but there was no sign it even got hot.

"All the more reason to find out where it came from." Bron dismissed the technician and went back to the computing section. The computer had already printed out the directional components and was engaged in comparing lists of known spatial objects which had occupied trajectory intercept positions at previous points in time. A mere glance at the time scale in which it was now seeking a match stopped Bron's heart a full beat.

When the final printout came he folded the paper deftly with the characters inside and without looking at them.

Let's see the answers, Bron. Ananias's voice cut sharply into his head.

"No. Let me hear yours first."

I'm not asking. That's an order.

"Get off my back, Ananias."

You b— Ananias's voice was suddenly cut off. Fragments of conversation followed too low in volume for Bron to catch. Finally Jaycee's voice came through.

Sorry about that, Bron. Ananias was throwin' his weight about. I don't think he'll try it again— not in that way. As we see it, there has to be a ship out in the void. The location of source tensor carried back to known spatial objects on the trajectory doesn't make sense. The only intercept is a location in Messier 31.

"The spiral nebula in Andromeda?"

No less. Travelin' at its subluminal velocity from

there would have taken all of seven hundred million years, so I think we can rule that one out.

Bron unfolded the printout. "All of which figures agree with mine. The Destroyer computer isn't bent."

So Cana does have a hellburner carrier way out in the void.

"It looks as though somebody has. I wouldn't be too certain it was Cana."

What you meanin', Bron?

"My dear Jaycee, Cana sent his crew to the Seminary because Haltern was due to take up his residency there. That was a reasonable action based on prior intelligence. But when that hellburner was launched not even Cana could have known exactly where in the Seminary Haltern would be at any specific time. In fact, the only off-worlders who knew at all times my precise position were Doc Veeder, Ananias—and yourself."

Ananias turned from the screen, critical disgust written broadly on his face.

"So much for your ability to handle Bron, honey-bitch. Let him break away like that again and I'll have you reduced to walking the streets—and knowing your poisonous talents I doubt if you'd make much of a success of even that."

"Jet off, you Godlost runt." Jaycee smoldered cobra-bright. "What you doin'—tryin' to drum up some pimpin' for the day you lose your pension?"

Ananias glanced involuntarily at the tabs on his shoulders. His small, pink lips were even more moist than usual and his bright eyes seemed to be reflecting some traumatic inner fire.

"Don't underestimate me, honey-bitch. I could do it, you know."

"Sick dreams, Ananias. You'll be lucky to retain your commission when Doc gets through with you."

The import of her phrase took a full second before it produced a shock reaction.

"Say that again—slowly, honey-bitch." His voice was sharp and suspicious.

"Don't play innocent. You know its against regulations to destroy recordin's of transfer-link sessions."

"What?" In his anger Ananias raised his hand as though to strike her, but forbore with the agonized realization that before his blow could fall she would probably have broken his arm. He forced himself into a more calculating mood.

"Who put you on to that?"

"Bron—askin' questions." She was enjoying his discomfort.

"And you told Doc?"

"Of course. I even booked him a call to Commando Central so he didn't get time to cool off."

"That was very stupid, honey-bitch." Ananias was struggling with his anger. "Doc should never have made that call. I carry the General Staff mandate—and that means I effectively outrank everyone on this installation. If it suits me to destroy some or even all of the recordings, neither you nor Medic-commander Veeder has any business interfering."

"You're damn wrong there." Veeder, entering

the door had caught the trailing end of the conversation. Although his expression remained within its authorized lines of concern, the reddening of his face and neck showed the height of his inner feelings. "I'll remind you, General Ananias, that this is a Commando installation and subject only to Commando control."

"And I'll remind you," said Ananias, "that you are engaged on a joint mission with Intelligence under a GenStaff Order. That places you under my jurisdiction. So far, I can't say I'm impressed with your handling of the situation. Honey-bitch has demonstrated lamentably little control over her agent and as for Bron himself—look at the kind of mental cripple I'm expected to work through: concussion, amnesia, schizophrenia and persecution paranoia—to say nothing of refusal to accept orders, insubordination and outright rebellion."

"You're a fine one to talk about mental cripples." Jaycee was furious. "Anyway, Ananias, where did you get the idea Bron suffers from persecution paranoia? I've seen nothing of it. It couldn't just be on part of the record you found it convenient to erase?"

"Honey-bitch," said Ananias dangerously, "I've already told you what I'm going to do for you. And as for Doc, I think premature retirement on a greatly reduced pension would still be more than justice. As of tomorrow, I'm bringing in Intelligence operatives to take over your function here."

"Drop dead, Ananias." Veeder subconsciously

adopted Jaycee's infectious mood of contempt. "At my request, Commando Central has verified that the operating arm of this mission remains under my control. Your capacity is purely advisory. As far as I'm concerned, you're here on sufferance."

"I shall contest that decision with GenStaff. You can't hope to win."

"Perhaps not, but while the order stands you will not destroy my records and you will not interfere with the operation of this installation."

"And suppose I do?"

Veeder's face broke into a taut glimmer of amusement, which was the nearest he allowed himself to approach to human triumph.

"If you do, General Ananias, you'll find yourself under close arrest in a Commando cell block awaiting trial by court martial."

"You couldn't hold me."

"I could—for long enough to see this mission through without interference."

Jaycee said: *"Touché!"* in a manner calculated not to improve Ananias's declining temper.

White-faced, Ananias turned to face the pair of them. For a moment it was uncertain whether he was nearer laughter or tears.

"You won't get away with this, you know. Within a week this unit will be entirely under my control."

"Don't need a week, Ananias." Jaycee was on the point immediately. "Any time now Bron should have the coordinates we need. That was the mandate, wasn't it—the establishment of the location of the Destroyer's baseworld? It's all over then except for the shootin'."

"Not quite over, honey-bitch. I'll have a few old scores to settle first."

Doc moved back to the attack. "In the meantime, Ananias, there are questions that need answering."

"Such as?"

"The goose-mutter which Bron heard—to which I would have attached no great significance had you not bothered to erase all reference from the tapes."

"And?"

"The question of how you could be so certain that Ander Haltern was the only Onaris technocrat who would interest the Destroyers?"

Ananias was fazed momentarily. "I thought that was all—"

"Destroyed? Not quite, Ananias. The transfer link to Antares is routed through Commando Signals. They also make recordings of everything transmitted or received."

"That will have to be stopped."

"You'll need a damn good reason."

"I have one."

"Then let's have it. The Commandos have spent nearly a quarter of their total budget for six years just setting up this project and my best agent's out on that Destroyer ship right now. If there are any facts we haven't been given, I suggest you give them fast. I'm damn sure Commando Central would never have agreed to cooperate this far if they had had a suspicion something was being held back.''

"There are levels of Security," said Ananias. "This one is out of the topmost drawer. The fewer people there are who know, the better."

"You're lyin', Ananias." Even Veeder was surprised by the vehemence of Jaycee's attack. "I know when you're lyin' because it's the only time you look human. God! Security's just a word you use for gettin' your own way without question—but don't be so naive as to try it on me. You're up to somethin' and it stinks."

"Honey-bitch," said Ananias, "you'd better keep a cautious tongue in that viperous head of yours."

"Jet off, you blackmailin' runt! Don't try threatenin' me. Don't you realize I could finish you any time I chose?"

"How's that, honey-bitch?"

"You fixed Bron's psycho-synthesis and the semantic recall triggers—but I had a few tricks with Bron extendin' way back before your time. Just one word from me could put Bron on the defensive—then he won't cooperate no matter what you do. How you goin' to survive that, Ananias?"

"Get away from those controls, Jaycee. That's an order."

"Go to hell, Ananias," said Medic-commander Veeder.

"When you've finished the infighting, perhaps

you could spare me an observer.'' Bron's mocking voice broke suddenly through the speakers. ''I'm going to try to get the coordinates from the subspace cavity.''

''Engaged.'' Jaycee forsook the argument and became quickly absorbed in rapport with the screens, her hands delicately trimming the controls by sense of touch alone.

''Full recordin' facility on, Bron. I'm followin'.''

Ananias shrugged resignedly and stalked toward the computer. Only when the ship coordinates had been firmly established and were ready for transpositions would he dare to interfere. But once he did move, the results would have to be swift, massive and final. There was no room for mistakes nor for the toleration of opposition at this stage of the game. Far too much had already gone wrong.

VII

THE CALL BOARDS began to chime the reassembly call. Almost imperceptibly Bron began to feel the additional components of gravity as the main drive was run up to full power. Watching the pattern on the board, he waited for the alert of the subspace team and gave it time to reach stations before he attempted to follow. It was obvious that the ship's present mode of gravity drive was merely meant to provide steerage for a fast subspace passage. The situation suggested that the matrices would be used as soon as they had been programed.

He was nearing the end of his time of waiting. Soon he had to pick up—either from the chartroom or directly from the subspace matrix—the coordinates that would betray the location of the Destroyer baseworld. At that point his own mission ended. The massed forces of the Stellar Commando, probably reinforced with the more spiteful dreadnoughts of the Terran Federation's combined navies, would split whole star systems apart if necessary just to destroy the world the Destroyers had made the basis of their might.

The battle would undoubtedly be the biggest space war in history—its winners would become a legend. Bron doubted anyone would ever see or hear again of a Commando called Bron who would have made the whole thing possible. At some point the incredible nemesis awaiting Cana and his forces would catch up with the Destroyer ship in which Bron now traveled and his end would come.

The lower corridors were almost empty and it was easy for him to pass through the minor gangways unobserved. Timing was important—he dared not be too soon and he must not be too late. Even now the subspace team should be setting up its fantastic and delicate instruments to define the two points in space between which the ship would leap into the tachyon quasidimension.

Although of a design unfamiliar to Bron's hypno-synthesis or his real memories, the entrance to the subspace installation bore the usual features dictated by the invariable principles of superluminal mechanics. The positive air pressure forced a gale around him as he opened the hatch.

In the access tunnel he allowed the cyclone air streams to swirl about him, the boiling turbulence removing the more gross dust and lint on his garments. Somewhere in his awareness lurked a familiarity with subspace mechanisms that bred caution rather than contempt. Not for a second did he attempt to disregard the elaborate precautions necessary to protect the delicate mechanisms in the cavity beyond.

At the tunnel barrier he exchanged his sandals for a pair of the soft, clinging shoes on the rack and carefully dragged on the flexible rubber suit, which clung to his body like a second skin. Although the suit was designed to accommodate a Destroyer uniform, it would in no way encompass his gown. He was finally forced to discard the latter and proceed with the rubber hotly uncomfortable against his bare body. He passed through the stinging detergent sprays and rinses and then the dryer. Only when this ritual had been carefully performed did he dare to penetrate beyond.

The anteroom, where the subspace crew would wait during the jump, was empty. Next came the labyrinth and beyond this the matrix cavity itself, always a place of darkness and wonder. Basically the cavity was nothing but a skeletal box between the great electrodes, surrounded by a gallery from which the technicians worked. Within the box, created and maintained by the field conditions which gave the atmosphere its green and awesome fluorescence, burned the billions upon billions of replica stars, a complete section of the cosmos in miniature. No illumination was permissible save for the luminescence of the field and the technicians were too intent on working to notice a watching shadow hard against the outer wall. Only their faces were visible, illuminated by the eerie glow, like a gaggle of witches engaged in some wild, black art.

With infinite care and delicacy the micron-straight, hair-fine probes were being extended like nearly invisible copper strands across the star matrix, defining positions and axes and measuring critical paths, probing always through the infinitesimally small spaces between the patterns of ersatz stars. Slowly across the micro-universe they were weaving the copper webs which would define the positions of entry and termination of their super-luminal jump through tachyon space.

Bron watched the work from knowledgeable eyes, his training or programing—he had no way of telling which—enabling him to assess the various criteria and thus the progress of the operation. Finally he judged it was time to move.

"I'm going to try to pick up the coordinates soon, Jaycee. I'll leave you to do the recording while I merely observe."

Engaged, Bron.

Bron moved slowly around the perimeter gallery. If he was noticed at all by the subspace team they must either have assumed he was one of their own number or else that he had legitimate business in the cavity. In any event, nobody questioned his presence, and the painstaking work of aligning coordinates went on without interruption. When Bron was sure the final settings had been made he cautiously inspected each gauge turret in turn. Despite his arrangement with Jaycee he silently filed the figures from the dim digital indicators into a mnemonic key as he went. Jaycee, for her part, verbally confirmed her reception of the sequences.

"I'm getting out now, Jaycee. I have to get clear before the crew leaves. I don't relish the idea of being trapped in here during the jump. Have you got all the figures you need?"

I think so. We'll transpose back into real-space coordinates and get them on transmission immediately.

Bron turned to negotiate the labyrinth.

"I suppose you'll be signing off soon? You've got all I came for."

We're scheduled to maintain contact at least until we get confirmation of the destruction of the baseworld. That's the GenStaff requirement. But I think Doc wants to keep the project going purely as a Commando exercise. Ananias has been playing a rather peculiar game—he's made us think there may be more in this affair than appears at the surface.

Bron was swiftly stripping the rubber suit from his sweating body. "Tell me in a minute, Jaycee. Looks as though they're going to jump fast."

Behind him he could hear movements in the labyrinth as the subspace crew vacated the cavity for the duration of the jump. He was well past the subspace anteroom, but still visible from its doorway. In the suit Bron had made an anonymous figure in the cavity darkness, but in his gown his identity was unmistakable. Only by gaining the hatch before the first crewman emerged from the labyrinth could he hope to conceal his intrusion.

Even as the outer hatch was closing he heard behind him a sudden buzz of conversation and the click of a communications handset. It was impossible to tell if this was a routine incident or whether he had been seen and his presence reported. Although his presence in the cavity in no way exceeded the license allowed him by Cana, the pattern of his interests was beginning to weigh heavily against his assumed pose as an academic syncretist.

Now that the Commandos had the information they required, Bron was free to try to mold for himself a pattern of survival if he could. Since he was sitting at what was calculated to be the losing end of one of the biggest projected space battles ever, his course was not easy to see.

The subspace alert broke his deliberations and forced him to look for safety straps. Most of the positions were duty points, soon to be occupied by crewmen. He found a spare harness near the communications room and thrust his arms into it. So tightly did the Destroyers cut their pre-jump schedule that many of the crewmen made their positions with equally little time to spare. Then the ship jumped. The Destroyers obviously believed in making concessions neither to ship nor men when dealing with subspace. They slammed into it at full power, hard, fast and straight. Thirty-three seconds of gut-tearing, bone-straining agony, during which their craft was slipped through the light-barrier to be hurled at superluminal velocities across the galaxy.

Bron knew from subspace theory what his conscious mind refused to accept—that by a process of involution the ship had in reality disappeared from the space-time continuum entirely and now actually moved between the webs of its own ersatz galaxy in the subspace cavity deep within its own guts. Stories still survived of spacemen who claimed to have seen the copper bars straddling the stars at the end of a subspace jump. Bron was not certain about this, but he did know that technicians caught in the subspace cavity during the jump had observed the ionization trail of their own ship speeding from web to web. Those of them, that is, who managed to recover from the shock.

The ship dropped into the quiescent phase of the jump and the tearing pressures eased. The heavy thunder of the grav drive was replaced by the eerie song of the fantastically delicate subspace drive. Bron unbuckled the harness and let it drop, finding suddenly that he was left with nothing specific to do but look for the one-in-ten-billion chance of survival.

His situation was unenviable. He could do nothing that might endanger the success of the Commandos—within these slim confines he was entitled to seek his own salvation. Yet who was he? Who was this parcel of human flesh upon whom so much seemed to have depended?

In the quietness of his own cabinspace the question suddenly seemed of great importance to him.

"Jaycee, now tell me about me. What name did I have other than Bron?"

None, Jaycee responded with quiet malice. *You were found in a street market of Anhatine on Bela-six by a Terran trade delegation. They had chartered a scudder and its descent blasted apart a pile of garbage. You were underneath, four weeks old. I wish to God they'd left you there, but they picked you up because they were Terrans and therefore soft and squeamish about the destruction of young life. They took you with them to the spaceport from which they were due to travel offworld. Neither the police nor the customs were interested, so you were shipped to Terra, registered as a demonstration animal. How you got the name nobody knows, but it was probably the coded customs stamp on your livestock export documents. In a way it seems rather appropriate.*

"You aren't lying to me are you, Jaycee?"

No, it's all on file. On Terra your presence proved embarrassin' to the dispersin' delegation. You were dumped in a para-military orphanage run by a Dr. Harvestine. Harvestine was a pathological bully, but apparently a good teacher. By the age of seven you learned enough of the brutal arts to break the doctor's neck in unarmed combat. Only the Commando school seemed to offer the type of curriculum to which you'd been accustomed, so the courts sent you there.

For the next fifteen years you took everythin' in the way of trainin' the commandos could fling at you. Both academically and militarily you persisted in comin' out on top. From weaponry through combat to higher mathematics you thrived on everythin' that was offered. But with one unalterable characteristic—a capacity for chaos.

"Chaos?"

Yes, Bron. The ability to play a system against itself until it breaks down and disintegrates. Then, when everyone is runnin' in circles, guess who moves through the ruins engaged in furtherin' his own ends?

"And that's me?"

That's you, Bron. Everythin' about you is chaos. Your personal life is chaos and the same thing happens to most of those with whom you get involved. You breed chaos and when the mess is thick enough you move in, pickin' the bits you think you want and then discardin' them when they don't provide whatever it is you're searchin' for. You do this with people as well as things—and without regard for the consequences.

"Tell me, Jaycee, did we ever meet?"

That's classified information, Bron. I can't answer you that.

"Damn you, I'll ask Doc."

You'll get the same answer from anyone. Our relationship is on a psychologically balanced basis and you or nothin' is goin' to upset the balance.

"Don't compute on that, Jaycee. If ever I make Terra again it'll take more than the Stellar Commando to keep me from the objective I have in mind right now."

The door opened abruptly and two armed

crewmen gestured him out into the corridor.

"Bron 'altern, Cana wants to see you. Come."

This time there was no attempt at respect. A curt order and a movement with a handgun were more an indication of an arrest than a request for company. Bron shrugged and turned as directed.

"This looks like the end, Jaycee," he said subvocally.

I'm bringing Doc on-line. If there's anythin' we can do . . .

"You know the only damn thing you can do is kill me to stop my breaking under torture."

The detail halted before Cana's door, motioned for him to enter, then took stations outside, handguns ready. Cana was seated at his desk, a solitary figure deep in thought, chin in hands, elbows resting on a plane of polished wood.

"Sit down, Syncretist," he said. "I take it you've concluded your investigations on the origin of the missile."

Bron relaxed slightly. "I have."

"Having checked a reprint of your calculations, I can assure you that your answers coincide exactly with our own. The fact that you programed the computer using a weaponry format rather than the classical software has not escaped my notice. One wonders just how far syncretism extends."

His eyes looked into Bron's with a questing comprehension that left Bron feeling weak. A slight smile surfaced on Cana's lips.

"You're a man of many talents, Syncretist. And I don't suppose we've seen all of them yet. But then, I should have expected nothing else from you.''

''I don't understand.''

Cana raised his eyebrows sagely. ''I take it you've already decided where the missile came from.''

''Of course. It originated either from a location in Messier Thirty-one some seven hundred million years ago or from a carrier somewhere in the void only a few hours before impact. From the location of your ring of ships at rendezvous, it is obvious that you know that a missile was going down on Onaris and knew in advance the precise details of its trajectory.''

''The implication being that the weapon carrier was mine and that the destruction of Onaris was an entertainment rigged mainly for your benefit?''

''You read me correctly,'' said Bron. Knowing both the nearness and the inevitability of death gave him a curiously fatalistic courage.

''You're no fool, Syncretist,'' said Cana, ''and you're no megalomaniac either. Ask yourself why the hell I would go to such lengths just to amuse you. The answer is that I wouldn't. To reach the truth of the situation it is necessary to make an inversion. We didn't anticipate that missile as much as it anticipated us. And its origin was in Messier Thirty-one.''

''That I decline to believe. Have you tried to examine the implications?''

''Yes.'' Cana maintained his intellectual calm. ''The implications are simply that seven hundred million years ago someone or something in Andromeda foresaw the precise details of our raid on Onaris and our acquisition of you and took steps calculated to prevent our meeting. So fantastic were their calculations that they were positionally exact and only about sixteen hours late in time. It's the same story almost wherever we go—but the time margin is becoming smaller. On present estimates we shall be able to get away with only four more raids. If we attempt a fifth, we shall still be there when the hellburner arrives."

"Suppose you leave earlier—or change your destination?"

"It makes no difference. It is the action we finally perform, not the decisions leading up to it, that is critical. If we plan a raid and abort our intention at the last instant, no missile appears. Sometimes nobody but myself has known of the intention to abort a raid—yet seven hundred million years ago that whim of mine was anticipated. If we plan a target, then switch to an alternative, it is to the alternative that the missile is directed— was directed—somewhere about the time that the first sparks of life were being struck in the Terran primitive soup. It's like the ancient concept of fate, fixed and immutable, that waits for you no matter where you run."

"Insanity!" For a moment the Haltern synthesis flared.

"Not insanity, Syncretist Bron Haltern—or whoever you may be." Cana's gaze was shrewd and unruffled. "Rather a matter of cause and effect. Initially we were primarily engaged in acquiring slaves, but among our intake was an inevitable percentage of indigenous intelligentsia. These we employed on high-level tasks. Sometimes a missile followed these raids and sometimes it did not. Our computers threw up the curious correlation between our acquisition of certain specialist technocrats and the destruction of the world from which they had been taken. These peculiarly fatalistic individuals all had knowledge and potential in one field of advanced cosmology—that of the patterns of chaos. Which brings us directly to you."

"In what way?"

"Seeing that our opportunities were running short, we made it our deliberate policy when raiding to acquire the best chaos men in the galaxy. Your reputation as an authority on the patterns of chaos ranks indisputably the highest and made you a natural candidate both for us and for the arrival of the missile where and when it fell. Only—"

"Only what?"

"The missiles normally consist of three cylinders at most. For you they sent seven. From a distance of better than six hundred thousand parsecs and seven hundred million years in time they must have held your achievements, actual or potential, in very high regard. What sort of things are you going to do, Syncretist, to realize that promise?"

VIII

A DISTURBANCE OUTSIDE the door forestalled any answer Bron might have made. Daiquist's voice could be heard raised in angry argument with the guard detail. Cana keyed a switch on his desk and the door swung open.

"Come in, Martin. They had their instructions not to let us be disturbed."

Daiquist strode into the room, followed by two junior officers. His face was red with fury.

"You've got that damned syncretist here—"

"Certainly." Cana regarded his fuming lieutenant speculatively. "What's on your mind, Martin?"

"He is. I thought he was a spy and now I'm certain of it."

Cana remained utterly calm. "You could be right, Martin. I, too, have my suspicions. But they may not be relevant. It's no accident that seven cylinders went down on Onaris. Spy or not, he's certainly a prime chaos catalyst."

"To hell with Catalysis. I don't trust him. He's too damned clever. He was snooping around in the subspace cavity just before the jump."

Cana stiffened. "Can you explain that, Syncretist?"

"I was interested in how you programed for the jump. I have some subspace theories of my own."

"I have other theories," said Daiquist, "and one of them is that you're not Haltern. It would take me only a half-hour in the interrogation room to get the truth from you."

"No." Cana's voice was sharp. "All the signs so far are that we've acquired in him a key piece of this entropy puzzle. Haltern or not, it doesn't matter much. He appears to have the potential to fill whatever catalytic role the patterns of chaos have already set. To put it bluntly, a large part of the future threatens to ride on his shoulders—and the future would be better supported on a fit back than on a cripple's."

"Then confine him to where he can't get into any mischief—or I can't be held responsible for your safety or the safety of this ship."

"Very well." Cana came to a sudden decision. "Break the jump, Martin, and put him aboard the nearest corvette."

Daiquist nodded his acceptance. "I've an even better idea. Let me put him on the *Tantalus*—and I'll go with him. I'd be interested in seeing his reactions."

Cana considered some hidden implication in the proposal, nodded his approval. "I doubt you're right, Martin, but there's a slight chance we might learn something. There has to be something very special about a man whose murder was considered so essential seven million centuries ago."

Daiquist nodded curtly to his aides. "Take the Syncretist and lock him up. One of you is to stay with him at all times. I'll have the jump halted. We should be ready to make transfer within the hour."

Bron was escorted to an empty cabin and locked in with one of the aides. He lay back on the bunk and stared up at the ceiling.

"Jaycee."

Don't talk to me, you pitiful cretin!

"What the hell's eating you?"

If they discover now who you are it could ruin the whole exercise.

"Spool the sermons, Jaycee. I need Ander, quick."

You need poisonin', quick. Ander's not here but I'll try to contact him. What's the readout?

"I want a fast replay on this patterns of chaos business. Maybe Ander can make some sense out of it, but I'm damned if I can. Was Doc in on that last sequence?"

On-line the whole way. When he'd finished his fingernails he started on mine.

"Charming. What's the general impression?"

As we read it, the only thing that's keepin' you alive is Cana's fear of somethin' else. God alone knows what that somethin' is, but it either exists or Cana's the biggest nut of the millennium.

"Cana's no nut. He's got a pretty powerful brain, but he's well balanced. He's at war with something and it isn't just the Terran Federation. So who or what the hell is it, Jaycee?"

Sometimes I wonder if Ananias knows. He makes like a seasick dog at any mention of missiles from Messier 31. He won't hear of the idea.

"I suspect there's quite a lot that Ananias knows and won't tell. Is he there now?"

No. He ran yapping to GenStaff with the coordinates instead of letting them go on standard transmission. I think he has ideas of taking you over personally. He hasn't been around long enough to know that workin' with you isn't the sort of job you volunteer for.

"I could almost wish he'd try. Any idea what kind of vessel the *Tantalus* might be? It seems to have some special significance for Daiquist and Cana."

Computer check through Intelligence records of known Destroyer craft shows no listin'. The only Tantalus *that shows up anywhere for the last fifty years is the Terran Army's deep-space laboratory ship that got lost somehow a few years back on an experimental voyage beyond the Rim.*

"See if you can get a bit of detail on it. Might

throw up something useful. I'd like a word with Doc if he's still there.''

Engaged, Bron. Doc Veeder's precise voice fell in soft contrast to Jaycee's edged tones. *What's the readout?*

''Assuming for the moment that Cana is right about the seven cylinders on Onaris being intended specifically for Haltern, don't forget that the man to whom they should have been addressed was Ander, not me. I don't know what a chaos catalyst is—but if Cana isn't mad or lying you could be sitting on some potential time-bomb-type events centered on Ander. I just thought the fact might have slipped your notice.''

It did. We were concentrating so much on your end that we had forgotten about the substitution. We're not yet convinced about this chaos business, but it might be as well to play safe. Any suggestions?

''Yes. Keep him well guarded and hold him available for communication over the transfer link. As I see it, something big is going to happen and he may well be the one person who can make sense of it all. I suggest you put a computer on full-time coincidence checking and feed every atom of even seemingly relevant data to it. This whole business has a decidedly off-beat feeling about it.''

I don't follow you, but I'll do as you suggest. I'll stay on-line for a bit in case anything new develops.

Bron relaxed and closed his eyes. The aide guarding him toyed with his drawn sidearm at the table. Both men waited in silence for the end of the jump and for the next round of action to begin.

Bron, his questing mind searching for some stimulus to bridge the hiatus, pushed his perception past the star static and the carrier hiss of the link circuit intruding from under his awareness threshold—and found something else. Something that, though he knew its shadows, he was completely unprepared to face—the goose-mutter, the phantom sound of liquid geese—but louder this time, nearer, and with an articulate and angry urgency that chilled him to the marrow. His mind's initial reaction was to recoil in shock, but his analytical faculty forced him to seek some explanation.

A glutinous, viscous, thixotropic foam of a sound, its incomprehensible yet meaningful babble struck him with all the implied urgency and horror of an unalterable disaster bearing down. Again his imagination fled, life-supported on an intangible raft, down the waters of some subterranean Styx, gathering shadows where there was no light and gathering sounds, the origin of which he dared not imagine. He felt the motion of the wash rippling gently at the breaking of some slight turbulence and sensed his own slow and measureless progression down the tunnel toward its end. What end? What lay around the dark bends of that terrible river? Fantasies more terrible than death reared up out of the shades of his imagination.

His unashamed scream coincided exactly with the shrill of the break-jump alert and a few seconds later the liquid geese were washed away in the intricate agonies of the end of the subspace jump.

Leaning past his escort as the tender left its monstrous parent's womb, Bron grasped the Hockung lens and brought it to bear on their destination. Space-worthy though she must be, the *Tantalus* bore none of the look of bronzed efficiency that characterized Destroyer ships. Rather she looked to have been dipped in whitewash that had lost its adhesion and bulged and sagged and stripped. Nor had she the trim outline of a naval craft, being squat and ugly and with a hindpart made hideous and complex by the devices of a dozen different drive systems. If her hull had once had her name emblazoned on it, the legend had long since succumbed to the attrition of space and to corrosion and pitting.

"Terran," said Bron subvocally, returning the Hockung lens to the navigator of the tender.

Check, Bron. Looks as though it is the Army's long-lost deep-space lab. There's a print from Records just comin' through, so we can run a comparison to see if she's been modified as a hellburner carrier.

"I doubt it. Even if she were capable of throwing a device like that I don't see how she could have achieved an accuracy of plus or minus a meter over that sort of range."

Somebody did.

From a closer view it was possible to see the effect of the ravages to which the hull of the *Tantalus* must at some time have been subjected. Huge pits and whorls had penetrated an arm's thickness into the metal in a manner suggesting she had been pressure-hosed with acid. In places the very metal itself seemed to have delaminated and the random curls and blisters of the outer skin in the process of detachment lent the ship a diseased and infected air. However, her docking equipment functioned efficiently enough and Bron, followed by Daiquist and the two aides, stepped through the lock into the warm, trim and quaintly outdated interior.

Bron stopped suddenly, his scalp prickling.

What is it, Bron?

"Something's awfully wrong here. This ship has a very queer feel about it."

What kind of wrong?

"The weird kind. I can't define it. Has the *Tantalus* been modified?"

Not as far as we can tell. But she did carry conventional weaponry—as do all Army ships— and these include Terran hellburners of the Nemesis class.

"The burner that went down on Onaris would have made the punch of a Nemesis feel like a love bite. Anyway, there was nothing human in the design of that damn thing."

Meanin' that you're acceptin' Cana's point of view that the Onaris burner was both aged and alien. She was coldly critical. *Why the hell don't you—*

"Spool it, Jaycee! I'm not accepting anything. I'm saying that if what I smell is right we're so far out of our depth that even if we sank at twenty-G acceleration we'd never touch bottom."

How do you compute that?

"I've just realized what's wrong with this ship. It isn't the *Tantalus* at all—at least, not the one that was built. It's a bloody mirror image."

Make a little sense, Bron.

"Look at the dials and gauges. Look at the labels. Everything. Lateral inversion complete to the last detail. This isn't a Cana stage trick, Jaycee. This is real."

Bron became aware suddenly that Daiquist was watching him with a fixed concentration that was actively hostile. Jaycee picked up the same point simultaneously.

Watch out for Daiquist, Bron. I think he's trying to use the Tantalus *to prove you're a Terran agent. Show any familiarity and you'll betray yourself.*

"Have the coordinates gone out on general transmission yet?"

"Don't know. Ananias isn't back. Why?

"As soon as the Terran task force is under way and the plan can't be jeopardized I may have to kill Daiquist."

Jaycee started to speak but quieted suddenly to allow Bron to concentrate as Daiquist turned back toward him.

"You're looking puzzled, Bron Haltern."

"This ship—it's not Destroyer manufacture?"

"No. Terran. A bit of cosmic flotsam we picked out of the void. It has its uses."

"Do Terrans always read meters backwards?"

"No. That's just a fragment of chaos. As a specialist in the field, it shouldn't perturb you unduly."

Bron broke away from the encounter with a shrug. Nothing in his own training or in the Haltern synthesis had prepared him with an answer. Daiquist's interest in pursuing the subject was broken as the subspace alert signaled the resumption of the jump. Unlike the Destroyer vessel, the *Tantalus* slipped into subspace with a mere shiver which was so soft as to be almost sensuous.

As they moved into the quiescent phase Bron began to get his bearings and started walking apparently aimlessly through the ship's main installations. He hoped an outward display of academic interest was in keeping with his pose as a syncretist. Inwardly he was looking for vital threads that might aid his own survival.

The *Tantalus* was a small vessel with perhaps only a hundredth part of the displacement of one of Cana's fleshholding spatial dreadnoughts. Since it was only lightly armed and, from its condition, scarcely capable of withstanding an attack, it occurred to Bron to wonder exactly what its function was in the fleet. Its laboratory facilities were well maintained and in use and it was crewed by an unusually high proportion of high-ranking technicians and even a few civilians. Their interest in his arrival ran in strong contrast to Daiquist's dour suspicion.

Daiquist shadowed him silently for a while, then approached and took his arm. "Come, I want you to meet the captain—Academician Laaris."

The captain was as untypical of Destroyer personnel as the *Tantalus* was of their fleet. His chart-room was a mess of improvised instrumentation, among which he moved with the agility of a sprite. He was small and dark and his bright eyes glinted with shrewdness. With only a formal acknowledgment of Daiquist, he forcibly crossed the veins of his wrist with Bron's in the Destroyer familiar greeting.

"Mastership 'altern, for you I die!"

Bron's surprise at the greeting must have been reflected in his face, for Laaris smiled broadly.

"No, we 'ave not met, but I know you well. Everyone who works on chaos knows you. The paper you gave at Maroc on Priam is almost our standard tex'."

Bron could not resist the question. "Is that what you're doing on the *Tantalus*—research into the patterns of chaos?"

"But of course." For a moment Laaris looked perplexed. "Is that no' why you come?"

"I don't think so." Bron glanced at Daiquist and waited to hear the colonel's explanation.

"Haltern's not here of his own free will. He's a prisoner and, we suspect, a spy. For that reason he's under open arrest. Watch him, Captain. He's a dangerous man."

Laaris's face was crossed by a bafflement which was rapidly replaced by a smile of relief. "The science of chaos is intergalactic. It is you, Colonel, who fail to comprehen' the liaison between scientific minds. Come 'altern, I will find you cabinspace. Later we can talk chaos."

In his new cabinspace, away from Daiquist's prying eyes, Bron's contact was urgent.

"Jaycee, for God's sake—haven't you got

Ander yet? Either I talk chaos with an expert or Daiquist is set to take me apart.''

Ander's been located, Bron. We should have him soon.

"Are the coordinates on transmission yet?"

Ananias has just come in. I'll ask—

"Put him on-line. Things are becoming critical fast.''

I don't trust Ananias near the control board.

"Damn you, Jaycee. Do as you're told."

Well spoken, Bron. Ananias's insinuating tones took over. *Glad to find I'm not the only one who has trouble with Honey-bitch.*

"Spool it, Ananias. Did the coordinates go out yet?''

That's GenStaff's business.

"And mine. I'm going to have to make a move soon. If I move too fast the whole Destroyer pack will scatter like a shoal of startled fish.''

You overestimate yourself, little soldier.

"No, but I underestimated you. Look around me, Ananias. Do you see where I am?''

On another vessel. Terran, I would guess.

"You're not guessing, Ananias. You damn well know. The Lab-Ship *Tantalus*, no less.''

Is that supposed to mean something to me?

"As I begin to recall it, yes. Are you listening, Jaycee?''

On-line, Bron.

"This amnesia seems to be catching. Run a re-play of the crewlist of the last recorded voyage of the *Tantalus*.''

Don't bother. Ananias's voice was swift and

angry. *I'll admit it lists me. But you've gone over the edge, Bron. I'm warning you to stay quiet. Don't be a damn fool.*

"Listen, Ananias, from now on this operation's going to be handled my way. You're going to cooperate, because you haven't the character to stand the stigma of being branded as a freak."

The sharp noise of a scuffle penetrated the transfer link. Then somebody screamed with pain.

It's all right, Bron. I'm holdin' him. He tried to hit the murder button, so I dislocated both his thumbs. Give us the readout. We'd better have the information this end so we can use it in case anythin' happens to you.

"Yes, you had better. Colonel Ananias, as he was then, commanded the *Tantalus* on the voyage during which she was lost. As sole survivor he made Terra two years later on a stellar tramp and claimed he was beaten out of space by a Destroyer task force."

It was the truth. Ananias's pained protest carried distinctly.

"I doubt it," said Bron. "The damage done to this ship was never done by any Destroyer. It's my guess you fled out of the void when something unnamable overtook you. I think you abandoned the *Tantalus* somewhere to make the story hold, then transhipped to Terra on a tramp. I hate to think what became of the crew."

You don't have a single shred of proof.

"I don't, but I think you have. Jaycee, you've probably slept with him. Was there nothing unusual?"

He's a Godlost weaklin'—but that's nothin' unusual. Jaycee's contempt was as sharp as a whiplash. *What you meanin', Bron?*

"Feel under his shirt, Jaycee. If my idea is true you'll find his heart on the right side instead of on the left—where it was when he was born. I think he became inverted at the same time as the *Tantalus*. And whatever caused the phenomenon had nothing to do with a human agency."

IX

BRON, I'VE GOT Ander for you.

"Put him on-line, Jaycee. He's got about five minutes to bring me up to mastership standard in the theory and practice of chaos."

Ander speaking. I do what I can. But I can only give you barest outline.

"Reading you, Ander. That will have to suffice. What is this thing called chaos?"

The whole spectrum of cause and effect, from the subnuclear to the galactic, considered not as connected incidents but from an entropic standpoint—as a random dynamic fluid.

"I can see the concept, but not how you can use it."

I come to that. First let me establish the importance of time as a factor. It's a fundamental tenet of the universe that entropy increases with time. The only exception is intervention by some form of intelligence, such as Man's, which can locally decrease entropy or accelerate its rate several orders above the norm.

A knock at the door signaled for Bron's attention. Shrugging his gown to the floor, he went to the door and opened it.

"Mastership 'altern, Academician Laaris would be please' for you to join 'im urgently."

"As soon as I have finished my ablutions I shall be ready." Bron freely amplified the weak suggestions of Haltern intolerance. "Tell him I come soon."

Securing the latch, he returned to the watcher in his head.

"Carry on, Ander. I read the words so far."

Don't need them, learn them. They're important. All chaos calculations are made against quantized time and can be either prognostic or retrospective according to the sign. They can be used to predict the future or to examine the elements of the past which have had a significant bearing on the present.

"But having randomized all your factors, I don't see how it's possible to determine anything by mathematical treatment."

Imagine a container of fluid.

"Your entropic system—molecules in random motion?"

Exactly. You should have been scholar, not soldier. The pressure of the fluid is due to the random collision and rebounding of molecules with each other and with the walls of the container. In the hypothetical fluid we call chaos the molecules are replaced by events and the events interact with each other just as do molecules.

'Keep going, Ander. I'm still with you. But I'm fast running out of time." Bron found the shower and ran it noisily. "Daiquist'll come looking if I don't show up soon. I wonder what the panic is."

I must lead you through this part carefully. Not understanding it could be fatal for you. Suppose your container initially had inhomogeneous areas of fluid at different temperatures?

"They would mix by diffusion. The energy of the system would remain the same, but the entropy would slowly increase."

Thus you have a fair analogue of the condition of the universe.

Another knock, heavier than the last, came at the door. This time Bron went stark naked and trailing water in his wake. Daiquist stood outside, stern, suspicious and angry. He seemed somewhat mollified to find that the promised ablutions were actually taking place.

"You're taking a damn long time, Syncretist. You're needed in the chartroom."

"The dust of the Destroyers is uncommonly hard to remove." Bron turned his back on the colonel and stalked back to the shower. Daiquist came into the room and stood impatiently.

"I'll wait until you're finished. You'd better hurry. Laaris needs you."

"Ander, this is going to be tricky. Keep talking." Subvocally.

If you can grasp the next point we're nearly there. In your container, what would be the effect of heating or cooling small areas of the fluid?

"Obviously local accelerations or decelerations of entropy." Bron switched on the driers in the cubicle.

And in our chaos fluid, what could be the only cause of the chaos analogue? I've already given you the answer once.

"You mean intervention by some form of intelligence such as Man's?"

Precisely, Bron. Home and dry. Events precipitated by intelligent intervention invariable lead to alterations in local entropy and these can usually be detected by entropic analysis. Going back to our analogy, this corresponds to local heating or cooling of points in the fluid. If it occurred in an actual fluid it could be detected in a number of ways according to its sign and intensity— optically, as a local change in diffraction; audibly, perhaps as an explosion or a cavitation implosion; physically, as a shock-wave or pressure difference.

"And in your theoretical chaos fluid?"

An effect similar to that of a spherical shock-wave spreading out from the point of origin— continuously growing, continuously falling in in-

tensity. It is observable only as minute ripples in the long tides of entropy. It's the inter-ripple and interference of these entropic wave fronts that we call the patterns of chaos.

Daiquist was pacing the floor angrily. He was obviously unused to being disobeyed and was distressed by an unstated urgency. Bron drew on his undergarments and then his gown, carefully subvocalizing so that his attentive antagonist should receive no sign.

"But how do you detect the ripples?"

Detection is the least of the problems. A detector can be as simple as an iron diaphragm in an oxygen atmosphere. Given a measuring system sensitive enough to show the acceleration or deceleration of its natural entropic change, it's fairly easy to see the ripples pass. But the mathematical analysis of these ripples into meaningful points of time and place is difficult.

Bron creased his brow. His conversation must cease in seconds and he would then need to adopt the pose of an expert. But he dared delay no longer. Daiquist drew his firearm and gestured for Bron to precede him along the corridor. Yet Bron's questions still needed urgent answer.

"Stay on-line, Ander. You spoke of cause and effect. I can see how you can locate the incident that was the cause of something, but what about locating the effect?"

The one is only the converse of the other. There is no difference between them except for the direction in which you read time. You'll be familiar with that concept from your studies of the fundamental particles. Both cause and effect make detectable entropic 'sparks' that become the centers of expanding shock spheres. If you can analyze enough of the sphere to be able to determine the radius of its curvature and its intensity you can locate the position of a cause or resultant both in space and time by extrapolating along the geocentric axis. But mark this: the significant thing about a linked cause and resultant is that those two correlated events, and those alone, will have coincident axes. If you can locate the one you can usually find the other.

In the chartroom the impish Academician Laaris had somehow lost his vivacity under a cloud of concern. Even his technicians, who had formerly shared his interest in the syncretist's arrival, were now too dumbly attentive to their boards to mark Bron's entrance. Instead of an air of academic interest, the atmosphere was charged with disbelief and panic.

"'altern!" Laaris almost split himself with relief on seeing Bron. "'altern, this you 'ave to explain." He seized a ten-meter length of chart strip and tore it from the recorder. "Such a chaos wave as this we 'ave never seen before."

Bron took the chart strip and began to explore along it. The multicolored lines started with slow excursions, gentle ripples on an abstract shore, part of the everpulsing patterns of chaos. Then a red trace broke away from its fellows, crossed the logarithmic scale to near infinity and was apparently arrested even there only by the inability of the luckless instrument to follow it farther. For several meters the errant trace fought the stop-post on the meter. Then, even more abruptly than it had arisen, the trace fell straight across the graph and disappeared below absolute zero.

Somebody said, *Holy Moses!* deep inside Bron's head.

Subvocally: "Did you see that, Ander? I need answers fast."

I don't have any. I need more information about the computer scan to be certain.

Laaris was upon Bron, almost dancing with im-patience to hear the sage explain. The Haltern synthesis stood mute.

"Academician Laaris, can you first define the parameters of your computer scan?"

"Scan? Scan?" The little man almost hopped with despair. "You don' need computer scan to answer tha'."

"You forget," said Bron Haltern coldly, "that your information is presented in Destroyer con-ventions, not mine."

"But always," expostulated Laaris, "the red line is your reference baseline. 'Ere it is the line representing this ship as a reference point. Where 'as it gone? Where went my ship?"

Ander said, *Have it now, Bron,* and began to pour information into his head. Bron considered the import of the words as he reread the last ap-pearance of the red line.

"You don't need me to tell you," he said at last to Laaris. "You know the answer as well as I. We have just entered a chaos-effect shock sphere and are proceeding directly down a coincident axis to the point of origin—which will be this vessel's complete annihilation."

Laaris looked up gratefully. "You, too, 'altern, say the same as I. I thought I was mistaken. Because I don' see how i's possible for the vessel itself to be on coinciden' axis unless somethin' aboard was also the cause of the annihilation."

"Curious you should say that," said Daiquist, picking up his gun and looking at Bron meaningly. "Because that's the one point about which I'd never had a doubt."

Daiquist motioned to a couple of the crew. "Look after the syncretist while I get this sorted out." He turned back to Laaris. "Am I to understand the chaos evidence means this ship is set for destruction?"

"There's no doubt abou' i'."

"From what cause?"

"That I can' say. The causal wave 'as not shown up. Perhaps if we reset the scan—"

"There's no time. I've seen how accurate chaos evidence can be." He waved an arm in Bron's direction. "Lock him up somewhere."

Bron submitted, reading the underlying perplexity on Laaris's brow and equating it with his own.

"Ander, tape me in, will you. We've seen an effect wave, but Laaris says the causal wave has not shown up. Can you have an effect without a cause? If not, why haven't we seen the wave?"

We will, Bron.

"What do you mean?"

It had me stumped at first. Laaris had a prognostic scan set up on his computer and was read-

ing a future event, the cause of which is missing. It's a highly unique situation even in chaos work, but it can happen. The simple answer is that the cause hasn't yet happened.

"But neither has the effect actually happened yet," protested Bron.

You're not thinking good chaos, Bron. The destruction of the Tantalus *is an event already fixed in the entropic patterns. It's impossible to alter that fact. But the means by which you are going to achieve its destruction have not yet been determined and therefore have as yet no precise point in the patterns.*

"The means by which I am going to achieve its destruction?"

Yes, Bron. You're the other end of the coincident axes. You're the catalyst that is going to initiate the entropic change.

"Not the Stellar fleet, then?"

No, or there would already have been a wavefront corresponding to their decision to attack. In fact, from the absence of extraneous lines I'd say the Stellar Commando fleet was not even going to get there.

Jaycee on-line, Bron. I just caught the trailin' end of that conversation and it computes straight. The Commando raid has been aborted. Disappointment weighted her every word.

Bron was staggered. "You have to be joking—"

The coordinates turned out to be Brick's World—an early settlement planet colonized durin' the Great Exodus. It's a farm planet, lackin' mineral resources. Definitely not a Destroyer

127

baseworld. GenStaff reckons the Destroyers use it for reprovisionin', but if they do they don't stay for more than a few hours. By the time we could get a fleet there the Destroyers could be anywhere in space.

"So the mission's a failure?"

We're going to keep riding with you in case something shows up, but officially the game is over.

"I'm glad you said that, Jaycee. I'm rapidly coming to the point where I'm going to have to take the initiative myself. Is Ananias around?"

He's down with the medic, havin' his thumbs put back in joint. Don't think he'll be doin' any maulin' for a few days. Doc's still fightin' GenStaff over him, but it looks as if Ananias might win.

"I haven't finished with General Ananias. There's a check you can run for me, Jaycee. Find out how much of the equipment we've seen on the *Tantalus* is Terran original. Ananias used to command *Tantalus*, so I want to know how much access he might have had to chaos information."

Which channel you readin', Bron?

"I want to know how much of this project he could possibly have foreseen, given the right know-how."

Engaged. I'll give you the readout as soon as it comes in. I could rather enjoy reducin' that bastard to a jelly.

The break-jump alert sounded shrilly. The *Tantalus* slipped out of subspace almost imperceptibly, in contrast to the subtle agonies of the Destroyer maneuver. Bron waited impatiently for release from the cabin in which he had been locked—he heard indications of the ship's being abandoned. At last the proximity lock responded to an unseen hand. Daiquist stood at the door.

"You have Academician Laaris to thank for this. I'd have been content to let you rot. But he was so impressed by your interpretation of his chaos graphs that he insists that you have the freedom of the facilities which he is unable to employ."

"Unable?"

"On chaos evidence, this ship is set for destruction. We've taken Laaris and his crew to another ship for safety. You'll remain aboard with a skeleton crew who will place the *Tantalus* into a safe orbit. If the *Tantalus* survives that long you'll be fetched down and held until Cana decides what to do with you. The skeleton crew has instructions to shoot you if you attempt to interfere with the running of the ship. Apart from that you're free to make your own way to hell."

Thoughtfully Bron watched the last tender leave. The only men who were left aboard the *Tantalus* were hard-lipped Destroyer shipmen, clannish technological animals, molded in the inbuilt ruthlessness that characterized Destroyer operations. Bron ignored them and made for the computer terminal, his mind beginning to play with the several possibilities the situation presented. Nevertheless he waited until the *Tantalus* was actually back in subspace before he dared to make any kind of move.

Actuating a programer, he began to key figures

into the input, working by touch on the laterally inverted keyboard and deliberately avoiding watching either his own fingers or the acceptance readout.

What you doin', Bron?

"Exercising my fingers. There are a few throats I've got to keep them in trim for."

Her voice grew taut. *Let me see those figures for the recorders. You know the rules.*

"Spool it, Jaycee. You had your run and it got us nowhere. Now jet off while I do it my way."

Are you defyin' me, Bron? Her voice was archly incredulous.

"I don't give a damn about you. Go ply your bitchiness where it's appreciated."

I said let me see those figures, Bron. I don't want to have to use the punishment circuits on you.

"Don't fool yourself. You'd just love the opportunity. It's the justification you're lacking."

She did not respond.

The program completed, he activated the transfer of the data to the computing complex unexamined, not wishing to expose his position by scanning the tape for the benefit of Jaycees' recoders.

I'm warnin' you, Bron. Perhaps you've forgotten what sort of bite I can apply.

"Call Doc, Jaycee," said Bron wearily. "If I've forgotten, he'll no doubt remind me."

He was now watching the intermediate readouts as the computer fled through the calculations. Over the transfer link he could hear Jaycee's voice raised in vitriolic protest. Then the voice of Doc came clear upon the air.

What the hell's this about, Bron. You should know better than to cross Jaycee. He sounded infinitely tired.

"Turn off the recorders, Doc, and listen. What kind of game is Ananias playing?"

You're not alone in wondering. He must have a personal deity on the General Staff to allow him to get away with what he does. In answer to your earlier question, it seems he did have access to a lot of chaos equipment.

"Was it he who suggested the Destroyers should be allowed to raid Onaris unmolested?"

Yes—but it was in accordance with the outline plan.

Bron watched the readouts with growing comprehension. "Was the Onaris hellburner in the plan too?"

No. That was something we hadn't foreseen. We wouldn't have let the Destroyers hit Onaris if we'd known about that.

"You wouldn't, perhaps. But what about Ananias?"

Naturally not—

"There's nothing natural about it—or him." Bron saw the "calculation complete" signal come up on the board and activated the printout.

"I have a theory that Ananias knew that hellburner was going to go down on Onaris and I think he knew it a long time ago. I think he knew it as surely as he knew where and when the Destroyers were going to pick me up. Don't underestimate Ananias. He knew in advance that the Destroyers' subspace coordinates would not ever lead to Brick's World.''

But they did.

''No, Doc, they didn't. Ananias double-crossed you.''

X

WHAT? VEEDER'S WRATH exploded like a bomb. *How do you compute that?*

"I memorized the subspace coordinates I got in the cavity on the other ship. I've just rerun the transposition to real-space terms. There's been no chance to consult the star catalogues yet, but I'd issue a written guarantee that the Destroyers' destination isn't within half a galaxy of Brick's World. The sector's all wrong, for a start."

Are you sure?

"Deadly sure. Ananias not only switched coordinates on the way to GenStaff, but he must have had a separate set prepared in readiness. Which brings me to the point of this conversation. However you may defend it, your Control center is the weakest link in the whole chain. I started a mission to destroy the Destroyers, and I intend to go through with it. I have a scheme and I'm going to try it. Doc, don't stand in my way."

Regardless of circumstantial evidence, Bron, you're still under orders. I admit the things you've told me need investigating, but you're to take no action unless I say so. Do you understand?

"No. I think Ananias is using you for his own ends. Since I don't know what those ends are I'm not willing to comply."

Don't take that attitude with me, Bron. We have ways of ensuring your cooperation.

"Spool it, Doc! Don't try to pressure me. I know the range of a bioelectronic transducer. It isn't even planetary, let alone interstellar, no matter how good your pickup."

Meaning what? Veeder's voice was sharp.

"Meaning that for you to receive transmissions from me or for me to pick up from you, there has to be a local repeater amplifier somewhere close. If I smashed that I'd be free from you until I came near the next repeater."

True, Bron, true. But you'd never find it—not in a million years. Don't you know how small we can make a repeater amplifier?

"Yes," said Bron. "It was just that knowledge that told me where it was. Now do I get my own way?"

You're bluffing, Bron. Not in a million years—

Bron fingered the crucifix hanging from the chain around his neck. He brought it up to where he could see the golden cross cradled in his palm.

"Now do I get my own way?"

This could earn you a Court Martial, Bron. You know the penalty for disobedience.

"Doc, do you think that threat holds any terrors for me? Try calculating the odds against my surviving long enough to come to trial."

There was a long silence, broken only by the blood-rush static of the pulsars.

All right, Bron. You win this round. We will watch and listen, but not interfere. Give me the information you have on the coordinates.

"Here." Bron scanned the figures rapidly for the benefit of the recorders. "You can rerun your own computation if you want a crosscheck. But you won't get it to indicate Brick's World. Don't bother to send any ships either. By the time they get there, there'll be nothing left for them to intercept."

I don't understand. You can't tackle a baseworld and a spacefleet single-handed.

"Just watch and listen," said Bron. "It's no accident that the *Tantalus* is heading for the end of a line in chaos."

You know I can't accept that, Bron. I have to act on this information.

"Please yourself—but the way I see it you'll never make it in time."

Bron returned to the programer and began to set up a new series of equations, occasionally interrogating the cosmological indices of the ship's

135

navigation computer when he needed further information. He worked now without attempting to conceal the input and readouts, knowing that other eyes were seeing what he saw, yet would be able to determine nothing without knowing his intention.

Shortly Jaycee came back online.

Don't know what you said to Doc, but he lit out of here like somebody put rockets in his afterburners. You know you aren't goin' to get away with this rebellion, you illegitimate worm. I'll teach you not to cross me if I have to kill you in the process.

"Get off my back, Jaycee. Didn't Doc tell you to leave me alone?"

He shouted to leave you alone officially. He didn't say anythin' about my speakin'.

"If this is to be a poison-tongue session, I'd have preferred the punishment button."

You'd have been better advised to do so, you abortive whelp of a sex-mad she-cow. How did you ever become so lucky as to forget me?

"It's a reward for good living."

Jaycee nearly choked on the point. *If you remembered what I remember, you wouldn't even joke about it. They don't make words to describe animals like you.*

Bron pulled the final readout from the printer and inspected it closely. Two doors from the chartroom he knew he would find Weaponry Control. It was unlikely to be manned by the skeleton crew, especially in subspace, but he would receive no quarter if the crew suspected his intention. Whether he had unconsciously subvocalized enough of his thoughts to warn Jaycee of his intention he did not know, but he heard her catch her breath sharply as he moved out of the chartroom.

The corridor was empty. Silently he slid along the wall, hoping that the door to Weaponry Control was not locked. It was not—probably an oversight during the recent exodus of technicians. He closed the door behind him and locked it securely.

When he was sure he was able to work without detection, he turned his attention to the weapon controls. Even in their laterally inverted state they felt familiar to him. His fingers were guided by a surfacing recollection of past weaponry studies he could not call to mind—yet they prompted familiar reactions in an ever-increasing cascade.

He knew then that his own memory was breaking through the block as surely as the Haltern synthesis was slipping away. He ran a quick check on the state of the magazines and was thankful to find them in good order. No less than four unassembled Terran Nemesis hellburners, small in power compared with the catastrophic engines that had torn Onaris apart, were waiting in the assembly ramps. All they needed was the armorers' signal, which would bring together the components to form them into the incredibly dangerous weapons they were. His fingers keyed the assembly sequence in such a short time that he knew he must once have been tutored by a master.

The automatic transfer of the missiles from the ramps to the firing tubes would be the most dangerous part of the operation. In the singing flight of the subspace mode the movement of such a mass within the ship was unlikely to escape the notice of the crew. With this in mind Bron made sure that the flight program was completely set and that the missiles' motors would fire immediately on entering the tubes. Any of his instructions could be countermanded from the bridge, but he was gambling on the fact that the missiles would be away before the crew could pinpoint the precise nature of his interference.

When all was set he activated the hellburners, then thumbed every alarm and repeater button he could find in order to create a diversion. The result was the nearest approximation to complete confusion he had ever contrived. The multiple blasts of various alarms racked the ship with a cacophony of noises. Every corridor was lit by a multiplicity of action signs, and the call boards began to chime for an urgent remuster, for which the ship had no available crew.

Remaining only long enough to assure himself that the hellburners were actually spaceborne, Bron headed back to the chartroom. Soon two of the crew appeared, searching for they knew not what order of disaster. They eyed Bron suspiciously, but went on hurriedly to locate the source of the furor some two doors away. Soon the urgency of the alarm systems faded and was followed by a peaceful hiatus. Bron studied star maps wearing an angelic expression and listening to Jaycee alternately cursing and bitching inside his head. But the tranquility could not last. The ship's men were not slow in deducing the cause of events.

Their leader was a tall and arrogant barbarian, whose mongoloid features youth made handsome in a striking way. His three companions were a mixture of races and traits that betrayed the inhomogeneous blood of the Destroyer nations and their lack of cohesive ethnic groups. They were probably tenth-generation descendants of the more reckless star-travelers of the Great Exodus who had flung themselves out to the farther limbs of the galaxy to populate the new worlds and create the new federations.

"You bloody insane, you make mischief after Daiquis' warn you." The leader signaled his armed companions into position with a mere movement of his finger. They were obviously a coordinated fighting team. "Now we're goin' make mischief back. You bloody Onaris Christian—le's see you pray."

This I could enjoy, said Jaycee, with rare anticipation. *Looks as though the boys are going to treat you to a little of their own kind of chaos. Trouble with you, Bron, is you never know when to stop sufferin'.*

"Pray." The order was accompanied by a blow Bron could have avoided only at the peril of drawing fire from the weapons of the others. He took it hard and fell. A pair of metal-tipped boots in his ribs soon persuaded him that he would find it less painful to stand.

"Now pray." The mongol was jeering. "Pray to me. Pray to me for your life, Syncretis'—because i's in my hands. Daiquis' said shoot if you give any trouble—but I don't think he'll objec' if I kick you dead instead."

Try turnin' the other cheek, Bron. He might die

laughin'. You don't stand any other chance.
Jaycee's ecstatic titillation made him cringe.

"Damn you for a vicious whore! One day I'll—"

A fist in the stomach doubled Bron forward and dropped him to his knees. As he folded, powerful arms seized his and dragged him upright again. The leader took his time about the demolition, using calculated swings to the head and body with fists that felt as solid as bricks. Jaycee played Job's comforter in Bron's singing ears with practiced finesse and relish. Bron took as much punishment as he was able before he felt his consciousness slipping. Almost thankfully he leaned toward the enfolding blackness.

XI

JAYCEE'S VOICE.
Perhaps it started as a whisper in some white wilderness . . .

The pain and the consciousness flooded back as the semantic trigger threw off the protective blackout. The mongol's eyes widened and a vicious thrust to the solar plexus made Bron scream with what little breath he still retained.

. . . a broken body, cradled in cold, cryin' futility unto a futile wind.

"Jaycee, for God's sake stop it! Let me go." He made no attempt at subvocalizing. It was as much as he could do to form the words at all. She was playing with him, deliberately using the trigger to keep him conscious so that his awareness of the torment would continue. Again and again the blows fell savagely.

. . . the mind 'mazed not by the searin' steal, the nibblin' nerve . . .

"Jaycee, in the name of pity—" He no longer cared whether he lived or died. All he wanted was release from the scientific and merciless battering his body was taking.

. . . some maimed martyr, crazed upon the cross, held up his head and cried unto the heavens: Lord, why hast thou forsaken me?

It was a full minute before he realized the punishment had stopped. Blood swam in his eyes and dripped warmly from his chin. He was still standing, but only by virtue of the arms that held him. Somehow he forced himself to appraise the situation. Two of the Destroyer shipmen were looking at something black and white. With difficulty he identified it as the Bible from his pocket.

The leader advanced again. Bron held his breath, knowing that a few more blows, even though they might not render him unconscious, must certainly fatally injure him even if they stopped short of his death. But the blows never came. Through one eye he was astounded to see that the mongol's face held a look of admiration.

"J.C.," he said. "Jesus Chris'. I seen many men killed by less beatin' than that. All of them wen' out whimperin'. But you still pray. I don' know abou' church, but i' make you bloody tough man. Wish you were fight on my side. You bloody indestructible.''

Dimly Bron discerned that they dragged him from the chartroom and even more dimly he felt a couch like an ocean of softness thrust beneath him. He was only partly conscious of the washing and the cool salve they heaped on his tortured flesh. But the one thing that burned in his consciousness before the blackness closed around him was the voice of Jaycee a million parsecs deep within his head saying, *That's only a sample of the tricks I can play on you, Bron. I'll teach you to get so lucky as to forget about me!*

He awoke in an unfamiliar cabin, sensing that someone had just left the room, but unable to explain the reason he thought this to be so. Not until the aroma of baked meats from a hot tray caught his nostrils was his suspicion confirmed.

Wincing with the pain of movement he thrust himself off the couch and staggered toward a wall mirror. There the bruised and broken flesh of his face formed merely a setting for the deep and haunted eyes that looked back at him from under swollen lids. He made his way back to the couch and sat examining the contusions on his body while trying to force the brittle meats past his damaged lips. Finally he resigned himself to the pain and dared to drink the hot, salt beverage he found at the trayside.

The food and the self-discipline needed to consume it rallied his spirits somewhat and he was finally prepared to meet the day.

"Jaycee?"

No. Veeder on-line. Jaycee's off doing whatever it is she does when you get her worked up that high.

"Spare me the naive approach, Doc. I'm feeling anything but trusting this morning. That must have been quite a party last night. Haven't felt like this since the morning after the last Christmas in Europa. Why did they let me live?"

I suggest two reasons. One—the Destroyers have an immense respect for strength and endurance. The punishment you took could easily have killed a man without your physique and training. Two—I suspect they haven't yet discovered the hellburners are missing. They returned all the controls in Weaponry to normal, walked out and locked the door. Being shipmen and not weapons men, they never thought to check the magazines. I don't know what you were attempting to do there, Bron, but you certainly paid for it.

"I'd have paid a lot less if it hadn't been for that hell vixen in my head."

They'd probably have killed you, said Doc sagely. *It was your fortitude and some lucky phrasing that saved you. I think you can thank Jaycee for your still being alive. We checked your new coordinates and you were right. The transposition gives us a primary and five-body system location which is only just in the advanced indices. A perfect setting for a baseworld, one we wouldn't ever have hit by chance. GenStaff has ordered the entire space fleet into the area. Estimated time is approximately one hundred sixty hours from now.*

The conversation was interrupted by the entry of the mongol shipman. He grinned at the sight of Bron's injured features and ruefully examined his own knuckles.

"You bloody head like rock," he commented sociably. He threw a Destroyer uniform on to the couch. "You wear this. You no' wear bloody gown. You trained fightin' man, no' creepin' Christian. I know."

This time Bron saw no point in refusal. The uniform was an excellent fit. The cut of the cloth accented his build and the width of his shoulders. The mongol, whose name was Maku, eyed him with some respect.

"You make damn fine Destroyer, bloody sure. Could use you any time I fight."

Bron said nothing. The shipman's understanding of him was intuitive and could not be dispelled by carefully chosen words. The charade was breaking down.

Thirty-five hours later the *Tantalus* dropped out of subspace for the last time, well clear of the limits of the solar system. The Lab-Ship held station, waiting for the rest of the Destroyer fleet to drop into real-space for the rest of the journey. The sight was not one Bron would forget. At one moment the *Tantalus* was a metal splint alone in the wastes of space. Then, one by one, the rest of the fleet materialized about her without warning and without other obvious effect.

The arbitrary point of subspace dropout in relation to the nearest primary would not affect Commando calculations much. A swift survey of the planets in the system would soon reveal the few that could be considered life-supporting. From there on identification would be swift and the retribution massive. Within days this area of space would become the mustering point for one of the largest avenging fleets of all time. Wherever Cana's ships went, the slight gravitational distortion trails they left would soon betray their passing to a thousand detectors and lead like a silken thread to the planet on which the Destroyers had homed. Curiously enough, Bron felt the avengers would probably be too late.

The subspace song was replaced by the thunderous vibration of the gravity drive as the *Tantalus* moved with its fellows. Although the shipmen were now busily concerned with navigation and the slow interjuggling as the overall command assigned orbit stations, they were never too busy to depute one of their number to shadow Bron as insurance against further mischief. Bron did not mind. He had no immediate plans and his relationship with the crew had grown almost cordial. Knowing the retribution he had placed in their wake, he felt almost sorry that such unquenchable characters as these were going to have to die.

He was sleeping when the final maneuvering diverted the *Tantalus* out of the fleet formation to a position well apart from the others. It was perhaps the cessation of the thundering gravity drive and its replacement by nothing but ship noises and the infinite silence of space that broke the depth of his slumber and threw him into an active dream state.

He lay no longer on the couch, but on a cushion, something as yielding yet as softly supporting as a woman's breast or the lining of a womb. He was moving, traveling on a dark, irresistible tide toward some terrible genesis. He could feel the motion plainly, the halt and turn of eddy and wash. He was conscious of unknowable pressures forcing him along, a peristaltic bulge cocooning his individuality, yet carrying him remorselessly onward.

There were noises, glutinous, coagulant, semiliquid sounds suggesting vexatious geese being drowned in a slow torrent of treacle. The sounds broke and foamed around his head, a frantic, frothy psalm, a submerged and harrowing hymn to halt the unalterable. And over all was the terrifying sense of doom, a great block of oppression like a ceiling of living lead.

Again he was making the journey down the awful subterranean tunnel. Again his intangible raft responded to ripple and eddy and he was able to sense clearly the dark and tortured path of the abysmal stream. As he encountered each dreaded curve he was possessed by the profound fear that this particular deviation would be the last. Somewhere ahead he knew with unreasoning certainty he would come to the end. At last the way would open out into some atrocious cavern and he would be borne, exposed and defenseless, into the presence of a reality he was completely unprepared to face.

Anticipation filled him with a nameless horror, begetting a rising panic that was enhanced by repetition of its threatened imminence. And ever the

147

liquid goose-mutter grew louder, more antagonistic, more agonized, more urgent, and more afraid. The babble was rising to a crescendo that threatened to force out sanity and replace it with something more alienly strange and fearsome than any delirium of madness.

The blast of a trimming jet close-by shattered the nightmare and broke him out of his sleep. As consciousness returned he sized up the situation and threw himself from the couch to the hard reality of the floor. He fell heavily, but actually welcomed the pain as a blissful alternative to his terrible wanderings. But though the visions fled, the goose-mutter remained unmistakable now as a background to the star static and the carrier hiss of the transfer-link transmissions that were ever in his brain.

XII

"DOC? JAYCEE? THERE'S that noise again on the transfer link."

It's neither of them, little soldier. They aren't here.

"Ananias? I thought you weren't allowed near the boards."

There are ways and means. Doc is apparently suffering from something that got into his coffee and Jaycee ditto from something in her alcohol. Since I happened to be on hand I thought I'd use this moment to come to a little understanding with you.

"I already have an understanding. You're a misbegotten, unprincipled bastard, whose time is very definitely up the moment I get within throttling distance."

What a great thing it must be to have a defective memory, Bron. As I recall it, there used to be two misbegotten unprincipled bastards and you were the more misbegotten, the more unprincipled of the pair. One might even say I owe my success directly to your malign influence. However, I didn't come here to swap compliments. I want to give you a warning.

"Jet off, Ananias. Nothing you say is going to make the slightest difference."

But it must. You don't remember it—but there was a plan behind all this. By God and guesswork it might still come off. But it won't if you persist in flying off at odd tangents on your own. Undoing those Brick's World coordinates was the stupidest stunt you ever pulled.

"That must have taken quite some explaining, Ananias. Very inconvenient for you."

That's nothing compared to the damage you may have caused. My one hope is that the Commando Spacefleet won't be in time to catch any significant portion of the Destroyer task force. Why the hell don't you leave well alone?

"What are you up to, Ananias? I don't know what you're aiming at, but it certainly isn't the success of the Commando operation."

Jupiter! Ananias was disgusted. *You're so far out of orbit it just isn't true. I'd be tempted to hit the murder button and start out afresh if you weren't such a powerful catalyst. I'm warning you, Bron, just play things as they come and don't start injecting any of your own chaos into the situation. If you attempt to foul things up again I'm going to have to stop you—even if it means blowing the whole thing wide open. Since you don't appear to remember much, I'll leave you with something to think about. Do you know precisely who cooked up those false subspace coordinates? You did. It took a twisted little brain like yours to work out that particular deception. And why? Because if those two fleets meet head-on they'll annihilate each other. And what the hell will we do then?*

Bron fell silent, wrestling with the wrongness of Ananias's words and unable to equate them to the situation as he knew it. He needed time to think. There was some activity going on near the central spacelock. Equipment was being readied in preparation for a ship docking. He stood and watched, impressed by the smooth cooperation and coordination of the Destroyer crew. These men obviously lived in space and knew it for the dangerous and relentless enemy it was. They were tough, uncompromising and thoroughly trained.

With a frown Bron realized that if these formidable Destroyers were to engage in battle with the Stellar Commando fleet nobody was going to win. It would not be a one-sided mopping-up operation. It would be a major running battle that would continue until one side or the other had been irrevocably beaten. And the few ships that limped home would be only the remnants of two of the most powerful fighting fleets in history.

Ananias's viewpoint made sense only if one took the view that the continuance of any spacefleet—even the Destroyers'—was better than no fleet at all. If one considered some common enemy . . . The sudden flare of goose-mutter in his head caused him to pause. And in that instant there fell across his memory the image of seven alien cylinders falling on Onaris from a distance of better than six hundred thousand parsecs and seven hundred million years of time. His mind spun at the immensity of his conclusion.

"Ananias, I—"

No answer.

"Ananias?"

Again no answer. The transfer-link board had been abandoned and for the first time since the inception of the mission Bron was utterly alone.

So concerned was he at his loss that he missed the beginning of some new phase aboard the ship. He was aware suddenly of a hardening of the men's manner toward him, a certain wariness untypical of their previous relationship. He guessed that some instruction about him had been received by radio and that he was now to be regarded as a dangerous prisoner rather than as the faintly amusing academic syncretist. Nobody immediately interfered with his liberty, however, and he was permitted to watch the docking maneuver as a trim, able-looking planetary ferry coupled with the *Tantalus*'s hull.

But once the ship-to-ship coupling had been made and the final abandonment of the *Tantalus* had begun in earnest, he was no longer left in doubt of his position. The tall mongol approached, directed a handgun at Bron's stomach. While he held unwavering aim he directed his comrades to attach wrist irons to restrict Bron's hands behind his back and leg irons to confine his walking. A pad of pungent somnific drug was held against his nose. Although he struggled not to inhale, he was unable to resist. Gradually Bron lost consciousness, slipped to the deck.

Maku regarded the fallen figure with something akin to regret.

"You no damn Christian. You damn fine fightin' man, bloody sure. Hope Cana goin' to look after you, 'cos Daiquis', him bloody insane." He looked back at his colleagues. "This a good man. Don' matter abou' which side you're fightin'— good man is all the same. The side you fight for is matter where you were born. The man you fight with is matter of choosin' sympathies. Damn sure him dead if he goes down in tha' uniform."

He kicked the prostrate form affectionately. "Bron 'altern, you no right to go to 'ell in chains. But right now we got to get you out of 'ere. This ship damn sure is set for destruction, an' Cana wants to make sure you don' to with 'er."

Bron awoke in a cell. His wrist and leg irons had been removed and with them the Destroyer uniform. While he slept somebody had carefully clad him in a clean, white gown and in his pocket the Bible hung with reassuring weight. The pallet on which he lay was undoubtedly planet bound, lacking the minute vibrations that characterized a shipborne berth.

For a few seconds he lay collecting his faculties before he hurled himself from the pallet in a frenzy of concern.

"Jaycee! Doc! Ananias! Somebody answer me."

The cell looked out through a small glazed slit to a gray-tiled corridor. The thickness of the door limited his field of view, but nobody was in sight outside.

"Jaycee, where the hell are you? Antares—if you have a monitor on this link, please call Control. This is an emergency—"

He looked around in agony for some way of attracting attention from somebody. The solid door made only the barest perceptible noise when he beat on it with his hands and the glazing in the slit effectively stifled his attempts to shout down the corridor.

"Jaycee—for God's sake—"

He heard a light groan over the goose-mutter and native mush of the transfer link

Weepin' demons! You aren't in the market for a planet-sized hangover, are you?

"Snap out of it, Jaycee. I've got to get hold of Ananias—"

You've got to get hold of Ananias? Jaycee was incredulous. *Bron, I've got first claim on gettin' hold of Ananias—and when I do you won't hear a thing for the screamin'. That Godlost runt put somethin' in my drink.*

"Damn your dipsomaniac misfortunes. Do as you're told. And get hold of Doc and tell him he's got to stop the spacefleet. We've all made a ghastly mistake."

He'll need a bit more reason than that to stop them now.

"Find him and I'll give him a reason. If those two fleets get together they'll wipe each other out."

Don't tell me you're gettin' cold feet just because you're sittin' at the center of the action?

"Jaycee, I'm a dead man either way. But I just realized we're fighting the wrong enemy."

Meanin'?

"That Cana was exactly right when he said he didn't put that hellburner down on Onaris. He doesn't have that sort of weapons capability any more than we do. That thing was alien and it came in out of the void with pinpoint precision to kill a planet of two hundred million people. Whatever creatures sent it in—it and the other thirty-five we've blamed on the Destroyers—they're the real enemy. If we engage Cana's fleet now we cripple both fleets and leave the galaxy wide open clear through to Terra."

If there are any aliens—what makes you think they're comin'?

"I can hear them over the transfer link. And they're the reason Cana had to build a strong Destroyer fleet."

Not agreed, Bron. Cana built that fleet to strengthen his opposition to Terra.

"Cana doesn't give a damn about Terra or the

Stellar fleet. Try to look at it through his eyes. If he had a weapon like the Onaris hellburner he could have put it straight down on Terra and forgotten about the Stellar Commando. He wouldn't have needed a major spacefleet in order to do it."

Point made, Bron. I'm puttin' out a red-alert call for Doc and Ananias. I don't think you'll convince Doc—and you haven't convinced me—but you do rate a hearin'.

"I rate more than that, Jaycee. I'm right—and you know it."

That's Doc's decision. Meantime, Bron, you're still actin' under orders. Don't try and break away again or I'll have to bring you back into line.

"I can't wait, Jaycee. I've got to warn the Destroyers to get their ships away from here. We don't dare let their fleet be destroyed. They're the only force already prepared and waiting for the aliens."

I can't permit you to move, Bron. Not until we see Doc's reaction on the spacefleet. He may decide we still attack.

"I wasn't talking about the threat from the Stellar fleet. I'm talking about a piece of chaos I cooked up on the *Tantalus* when I thought the spacefleet wasn't going to get here."

Why? What the hell have you done? Jaycee's voice was as hard as diamond.

"Done? Jaycee, I arranged the destruction of this whole planetary system."

Spool the drama, Bron. You didn't have the hardware for that sort of action.

"I did, Jaycee. I had the hellburners—I fired them from *Tantalus* in subspace. I precalculated their subspace drop-out position and programed their subliminal trajectory from there. They're due to arrive on target very soon now."

There's still no panic. Four Nemesis hellburners won't touch a space fleet in orbit. They won't do more than blacken a couple of continents.

"They can if you use them right. It isn't just the baseworld that's going to go—but everything on the three inhabitable planets of this system."

Stop tryin' to pressure me, Bron. I know you're Satan incarnate, but not even you can do that with four small hellburners. Anyway, the Destroyers could see them comin'.

"Not where I sent them. On such a long approach trajectory they'd normally be detected and intercepted as soon as they came within attack range. Mine weren't programed ever to enter attack range."

"Then where the hell did you send them—into the primary?"

"No, their effect would have been negligible on a sun. But there are six planets in this system, of which this is the third. The neighbor to sunward and the one spaceward are also inhabitable, according to the Destroyer cosmological index on the *Tantalus*. But the innermost planet is too close to the sun and too dense to support life. It's half molten and extremely friable. The hellburners are programed to go down on that."

They'll split it apart and . . . The last part of the

sentence was lost as the implications of the situation swamped Jaycee's powers of credulity. *But if any substantial part of it comes out of orbit and goes sunward you'll get a flare that will sterilize the whole system.*

"If my calculations are correct," said Bron, "almost the entire mass will go sunward. I've got to warn the Destroyers to pull out. I want an FTL transmission put out at full power from Antares on the Destroyer emergency wavebands. Get me Antares on-line."

Bron, you know I can't do that without Doc's authorization—and even he'd have to clear it through GenStaff.

"There isn't that much time available. By the time GenStaff came up with a decision it would all be over."

He went to the cell door and beat on it with his hands.

"Damn it, Jaycee, if you won't warn the Destroyers I'll have to find some way to attract their attention from here."

Don't try, Bron. You're still under orders and those orders still say the Destroyers are the enemy. If you attempt to warn the Destroyers it'll be mutiny. I'll stop you by any means I have.

"Get off my back, Jaycee."

He slipped down and explored the bottom of the cell door with his fingers.

Don't try anythin', Bron. You've already jumped out of line once and had a beatin' taken out of your skin. Don't you ever learn?

"Do me a favor, Jaycee—drop dead."

A small light fixture in the ceiling attracted his attention and gave him an idea. His hand brushed the Bible in his pocket and he took it out and examined it eagerly.

Its material appeared excellently flammable. The metal bunk on which he had lain was his next objective. Fortunately it was not strongly secured to the wall. He wrenched it free.

I'm warnin' you, Bron. If you cross me this mornin' I'll kill you. I'm in no mood for your God-lost games.

"Stay out of my hair, Jaycee. You don't dare hit the murder button and none of the others is going to stop me."

Bron lifted the bunk and smashed the protective transparent shield away from the solitary light. The light itself faltered but did not go out.

I don't know what you're up to, Bron, but quit now. I warn you I'm just in the mood to give you a taste of the punishment circuit.

"You'd enjoy that, wouldn't you, Jaycee?" Bron smashed the solidstate lamp away and the cell fell into darkness save for the dim illumination that came in through the slit in the door.

God! Enjoy it? You don't know how near I come to usin' it sometimes. Just out of—

"Spite?" With the bunk on its side and with careful balance, Bron could just about reach the small wires he had exposed in the broken lamp fitting.

Spite—revenge—hatred—I don't know what

the hell you induce in me.

A careful twist of the fine paper torn from the Bible aligned in the dimness between the wires ought to kindle to a spark, Bron thought. Another single sheet would give him scant protection against the current, but he dared not use more in case he damped the arc. There would probably be only one chance before the circuit protectors cut the current.

Bron, I'm warnin' you . . .

"Why don't you press the button, Jaycee? If it'll really give you satisfaction." Under his fingers the spark flared briefly but enough for ignition. A flame leaped up between his fingers as the dry paper caught fire. He jumped carefully down from the edge of the bunk and began to pile page on separated page on the small fire he was making on the floor.

Oh God, Bron—the urges you rouse in me—

Bron successfully transferred a blazing sheet of paper to the door and pushed it under. He had no means of knowing whether the flame survived, but he fed more sheets beneath the door and hoped at least for smoke to stir some alarm system into operation.

"Press that button, Jaycee, you vindictive bitch. If you dare. I'd be interested to know what it does—to both of us."

Prepared as he was, the pulse of pain that hit him was far greater than he had imagined possible. Almost every sensory nerve in his body seemed to contribute to the pillar of corroding agony that possessed him. Even when the pulse was gone he lay for a full half-minute trying to erase the memory of those seconds. When he tried to speak his vocal cords were taut and the words would not come out.

But he did not need to speak. Jaycee's near hysteria came through clearly against the background of goose-mutter and the blood-rush of the pulsars. He decided ruefully that those thirty seconds had cost Jaycee quite as much as they had cost him. Her distraught voice flared in his head. *. . . you contaminate me, Bron. You twist everythin' that's in me. Damn you—damn you . . .*

When the second pulse of pain began he knew from the sobbing that her finger was going to hold that button down for a long, long time. Perhaps until Doc or Ananias came and pulled it off. Fortunately she was too distressed to think of using the semantic trigger this time and mercifully he passed out where he lay.

XIII

HE CAME AROUND spluttering. The Destroyers had thrown water in his face. He was no longer in the cell, but on the floor of some kind of communications room ringed with consoles. Daiquist, his face full of thunder, stood astride him, looking down. Cana stood to one side, his powerful intellect still striving to come to terms with the full implications of the situation. Bron struggled to his feet, puzzled by the open accusation in their eyes.

Daiquist swore. He said, "I admire your nerve,

but this is the last trick you'll ever pull. And to think we carried you out from Onaris—'' Words failed him, as if some yet unexplained glimpse of Bron's deception were a revelation greater than he could express.

"I don't understand you." Desperately Bron tried to maintain his cover, but he knew instinctively that his cause was lost. Yet how? Why? Daiquist's suspicions had hardened to a certitude, but the factor responsible for Bron's suddenly altered status was not apparent.

"What the hell's gone wrong, Jaycee?" Subvocally.

Ananias has sold you out, Bron—Her voice was dull and leaden. The sentence continued, but Bron was no longer listening to the words. He knew all too suddenly what had gone wrong. As well as coming from the transducers in his head, Jaycee's voice was issuing over the Destroyer's loudspeakers.

Daiquist's smile was a mixture of triumph and malice.

"Now, Syncretist—do you still fail to understand what I'm talking about? You and that on-line Commando bitch? We've learned quite a lot about you in this last half-hour. So she wants you to suffer? Well there I can certainly oblige. You're going to suffer as nobody has ever suffered before. By the time I've finished with you I doubt if even the Stellar Commando will have stomach enough to send us another spy."

"If you were able to hear us," said Bron,

"you'll know that I was trying to attract your attention. Those hellburners I sent to the first planet—you've only got hours to get away before the sunflare."

"Judging from the extent of your deception this far I suspect this as just another trick. It would be only too convenient for the Commando if we abandoned our defensive position and scattered our ships right into the face of the approaching Stellar spacefleet."

"It's no trick," said Bron. "I had no idea you could monitor our transfer link."

They didn't need to, Bron. Ananias took to space in an Intelligence radio ship. It seems he's interceptin' our transfer link and rebroadcastin' it through Antares on FTL radio over the Destroyer emergency wavebands.

Cana shot a quick look at a radio technician at one of the consoles.

"Is that true?"

"FTL transmissions on our emergency bands, damn sure."

"It could still be a trap," said Daiquist sourly. "I'm going to take him apart the hard way. I'll make him plead to be allowed to talk."

Cana held up his hands. "No, Martin. If it is a trap—at least the Stellar spacefleet won't catch us unprepared. We can clear this system in battle formation and meet them on equal terms. But my instinct tells me there's no trickery involved."

"How do you arrive at that conclusion?"

"Because the chaos patterns predict the destruction of the *Tantalus*. You heard where the Syncretist said he had directed the Nemesis hellburners. Now tell me what you've done with the *Tantalus*?''

"It's abandoned in orbit around the first planet."

"And can you think of a more probable catastrophe that can happen to it than the one he has described?"

"No—" Daiquist's face expressed the measure of his agonized indecision. "But I still think I'd better take him—"

"Don't you understand?" Cana turned on him the full force of the personality that held a whole federation of rogue planets to heel. "Martin—if the Syncretist is right, we'll all be dead before you get your answers."

"Then just let me kill him. I don't fancy going into battle with the enemy having a direct intelligence link in our midst. Regardless of what the patterns say we've already taken chances enough."

"No, Martin. I can't permit it—and you know my reasons." Cana turned to Bron. "I've got the greatest reservations about you, Commando or syncretist, whichever you may be. The only reason you're still alive is that whichever way we plot the patterns of chaos we always seem to find you at the causal focus of some of the most aggressive waves. Apparently you're the catalyst calculated to initiate some of the most violent entropic upheavals the universe has ever know. So answer me this, Bron Haltern, or whoever you may be—just how do you intend to take up the cosmos and twist it by the tail?''

A sudden clatter came from one of the monitoring consoles and an operator cried out in surprise.

"The *Tantalus*, sir. She 'ave stopped transmittin'. I think she bloody destroyed.''

Cana looked at Daiquist sharply. "Can you still doubt the patterns, Martin? That's the hellburner's strike on the first planet. It could take hours for the fragments to reach the surface of the sun, but the consequent sunflare will only take minutes to reach us. Order an emergency evacuation.''

"I still think it's a trick.''

"Trick or not, can you still doubt the Syncretist's ability to influence events on a cosmological scale?''

Daiquist was growing angry. "Look, Cana, what's to stop me from shooting him where he stands? If I put a shot through him now, what of the patterns then?''

"An interesting speculation, Martin. Since his effectiveness is already included in the patterns, either you will be prevented from touching him or we should gain first-hand knowledge of resurrection. Either way offends my materialistic dignity, so I forbid you to try. I'll take him with me to the flagship, while you organize the evacuation. We have a system to lose and a fleet to save, so there's no use in arguing now.''

With bad grace Daiquist turned to the radio operator at the console.

"Order a general alarm. All personnel to return to their ships and all ground staff to remuster for emergency evacuation. All ships to be placed in battle readiness fourteen system diameters out. This is a prime emergency and there will be no repeat of this instruction."

Daiquist moved across the room, now shouting detailed orders. Cana looked at Bron sagely.

"Well, Syncretist, do I take you in chains or do I have your word that you will attempt no further mischief? In any case I ought to know your Commando rank."

"I can give you neither. First, I'm still on active service under control of Commando Central. Therefore I can give you no personal assurances. Second, I've forgotten my rank along with most other details of my personal life."

"Then perhaps your mentor would be so good as to supply the information?"

He's Commander Bron, of the Commando Central Intelligence Bureau, supplied Jaycee dully.

Cana's eyes widened appreciably and he smiled as if at some old memory. "Ah yes! I might have guessed. Tell me, Commander, does she hear me through you?"

"Not only hears you—she can also see you."

"Remarkable." Cana's eyes instinctively searched Bron's head but learned nothing of the transducers buried deep into the skull. "I had underestimated the Commandos both for their technology and for the class of men they produce. Nevertheless I shall still have to think of you as Haltern the Syncretist, because that is undoubtedly the catalytic role you have to play. Shall we go?"

Escorted only by Cana's aides, they went through a door and were suddenly in the open air, standing in a pale-gray light of what Bron took to be early dawn. Looking about him, he could see nothing but a stretch of sparsely vegetated waste-land stretching as far as the eye could reach. The air was damp and chill and inhabited by a forlorn sense of loneliness—the antithesis of what he would have expected from a Destroyer baseword. Only the cleaved rock of the buildings they had just left suggested the works of man.

Initially he was perplexed by the barren out-look. Then his estimate of the pale sun sharpened when he saw the height of its position. He knew then that this parody of winter was all the noon this blighted place was going to get. Nobody would build a baseworld in a place so inhospitable and where the ecology was so starved of the essential energy for photosynthesis. The more he thought about it, the more obvious the situation became. The Destroyer flesh-ships had not been making directly for their baseworld, after all. They had needed to unload their cargoes of flesh upon what-ever world they had chosen to be worked. This was a mere colony world—a labor camp for the thousands of slaves who were to have been tossed upon its barren soils to work out their lives under a sparse and alien sun.

Men were cheaper than machines for initial col-onization. They were more easily obtained, more versatile. They had the gift of self-duplication, which was not a feature of mechanisms, and, though vastly less efficient, they could be made to perform any labor a machine could do. It mattered little how many of them died in the fields, since a nurtured nucleus could always be used for breeding further stock. Thus, in the broadest economic sense, mankind had even yet triumphed over automation. Machines cost money and skilled attention: slaves cost no more than their transportation and the cost of the whips to drive them to the fields.

Bron felt suddenly sick. It was upon this gray wraith of a world that he had called down a vengeance to end all vengeance. The Destroyer fleet was still in orbit and the only craft visible were ferries. With the great spacefleet above preparing for battle with the approaching Commando fleet, it was a certainty that the hapless Onarian slaves would be hastily dumped on the planet's surface to await the ordered coming of the sunflare that would sterilize the planet and everything that remained upon it.

He was aware that Cana was studying him closely and he wondered if the great Destroyer's intellect could extend to an appreciation of his captive's thoughts at that moment. If it did, Cana showed no sign. His features were hard with the granite resolution of a man who had been forced to perform impossible tasks and had even more impossible tasks yet to perform. It was the face of a man whose visions were cosmic in content.

Dotted about the far fields were the blunt ferry ships which formed the planetary link with the orbiting spacefleet. Around them a score of scudders swarmed like gnats, fetching and carrying services and personnel, hovering uncertainly, then darting swiftly to their destinations as the message of urgency spread among them. Occasionally new ferries would land and others depart. Groups of bewildered Onarian slaves were being driven to the wasteland and the ships refilled with Destroyer land crews hastily called back to join the battle fleet.

Many long and anxious glances were directed toward the gray myth of a sun that might suddenly redden and expand to the dreaded sunflare. For one terrible moment this sad, pale world would know a summer more splendid than anything in its history. But accompanying the warmth and the light would come the bands of radiation and the increasing heat that would dry the seas, scorch the land and finally melt even the stubborn rocks for many kilometers down. Its happening was a predictable certainty, but the timing of the event was a matter about which nobody could be precise.

Bron, too, was possessed by a rising measure of concern—as if the cataclysmic nature of the impending doom held a psychological weighting that transcended his purely personal fear of death. His attention was drawn by a burst of activity as a new ferry landed nearer than the rest. Seven open-topped scudders, flying low with a deafening scream of engines, dropped in formation across the wasteland and halted only meters away.

Cana motioned to Bron to climb aboard one of

the craft, then turned back to look for Daiquist. He waited several minutes, looking alternately at his watch and at the sun, while a scudder pilot made frantic efforts to establish contact with Colonel Daiquist over the radio. Cana and Bron were joined by an increasing number of Destroyer personnel evacuating the nearby buildings. As each scudder became loaded to capacity Cana waved it away, indicating his preference to wait for a later craft. Since Bron was already seated in a scudder he found himself in a knot of anxious shipmen being whirled to a waiting ferry well in advance of Cana's own transport.

Clad as he still was in the white robe and moreover, the known author of the current crisis, Bron could well have expected a high degree of antagonism from the Destroyers in whose company he had been thrown. Instead he encountered the respect due a highranking Destroyer officer. Steps were provided to enable him to dismount from the scudder when the ferry was reached and on the vessel itself his safety harness was made ready for him.

After a seeming eternity the ferry lifted off, climbing rapidly under the hands of a skilled crew, confident even in an emergency. The docking with the mother ship was precise and Bron had the feeling that he had never seen similar action performed more professionally by any Commando crew.

A courier was waiting to take him to the ship's bridge. Cana arrived there at about the same time.

Almost immediately the ship began to throb with the overall thunder of the main gravity drive. The energy with which the drive was applied suggested that the ship's departure from its orbital station was a matter of crash urgency. Cana thrust him near one of the great navigational viewscreens and Bron could see precisely what the urgency was.

He caught his breath as he gained a comprehension of the awesome sight. The scanners were trained on the sun upon which the little gray world had depended. But this sun was sparingly benevolent no longer. Broadly across its center spread a sunstorm of such frightening intensity that, even viewed from the ship's present distance of better than a hundred million kilometers, its ferocity seemed to threaten to engulf all. But the boiling, granulated ferment of the storm was nothing compared to the astonishing outrush of the flaming, eruptive prominences, spreading probably at a tenth of the speed of light like fantastic, feathered nuclear flames. The whole sun appeared to contract and then to swell and to belch out its infinitely hotter interior fires with such hellish virulence that the scanners had repeatedly to attenuate their reception of the scene in order to compensate for the spiteful increases in luminosity. And as the pulsing brilliance increased, so the feathered fingers of the sunflare fled farther and farther out into the massive volumes of space.

It was impossible for Bron to judge the scale at which the boiling ebullition was portrayed, but the scanners panned repeatedly away from the initial scene in order to contain the rapid progress of the flare as it spread across the system. In advance of the visible extension, the vast increases in cosmic and ultraviolet radiation must already have punished the shielding atmospheres of the inhabitable planets beyond endurance. Even in this short time the second world must have become an irradiated hell. The third planet, which Cana had only just abandoned, must be under such a bombardment from the skies that life outdoors would be impossible and life indoors meant slow and certain death from the effects of primary and secondary radiation. The rapidity of the cataclysm far exceeded anything Bron had imagined.

Occasionally the scanners picked up images of Destroyer ships, remote splinters of darkness against the brilliance of the spreading holocaust. Each ship was engaged in a long, forced trajectory its command hoped would clear it of the planetary system and take it to a point beyond the corrosive fingers of the enraged sun.

The scanners swooped down to concentrate in detail on the third planet. The groan of anguish was audible. Seven Destroyer ships were still in orbit and most probably would remain so. Bathed in such a concentration of deadly radiation, it was certain that even their magnificent shielding could not prevent the destruction of their crews.

From somewhere on the surface, a ferry staggered into the sky, then lost control and, its drive still raging, nosed down again in a horrifying power dive to the planet's surface. Cana called for more detailed views and one by one the orbiting ships were scanned and identified. None of the trapped ships betrayed any possibility of being able to move and only a little more time would ensure their complete sterilization. One day, perhaps, it would be possible to reclaim the vessels. For the men who had taken the ships to the far corners of the galaxy there was no hope at all.

Cana's flagship, *Skua,* fled well in advance of the grasping radiation fingers and soon the thundering urgency of the gravity drive relaxed to a normal pitch. But Cana himself signaled no such relaxation. His quiet anger still ran with a tide of energy frightening to behold. He called repeatedly for figures and data on the ships that got away—and on the ones left behind. Finally he turned to Bron with a wrath that seethed like a cauldron only a hair's breadth beneath the surface of his iron composure.

"Do you know what you've done to me, Syncretist? You've cost me three inhabitable planets, at least seven ships, better than a thousand men—and Martin Daiquist." He paused for a moment as words seemed to fail him. Then he continued, again fighting to prevent his anger from breaking surface.

"One man, a bloody book and a headful of bio-electronics. Zeus! No wonder the patterns of chaos treat you with such respect. If this is what you can achieve as a prisoner—I shudder to think what could happen to the universe if they gave you a fleet."

He turned his head sorrowfully in the direction of the screens now filled by a swollen and distorted sun which had been provoked into destroying the satellite planets it had nurtured for so many millennia. "First I have to ensure my fleet is safe. Come to my cabin in an hour, Syncretist. We shall have a great deal to talk about." He walked away, calling for a conference of ships' captains and cursing the communications men who were fighting a losing battle with fierce electrical storms in an effort to maintain vital radio links in the face of an angered star.

Bron lingered by the screens, still overwhelmed by the enormity of the havoc he had caused. Destruction on such a colossal scale using only four small Nemesis hellburners had been possible only because the perverse genius of his own mind had given him an idea that had magnified the normal potential of the weapons a millionfold or more. But he was not alone in appreciating his own talents for violent destruction. Somehow the dark entropic echoes of even more violent things he had yet to do were already throbbing their way through the continuum. He was facing a pre-destiny so immense in its effects that his assassination on Onaris had been ordered seven hundred million years ago in another island universe, far across the terrifying voids of space.

XIV

JAYCEE SPOKE IN a quiet voice, intruding on his reverie. *Doc reckons you were lucky the sun didn't go nova, Bron.*

"Doc's back?"

He's been back for hours—replayin' the tapes and tryin' to get some answers.

"Answers to what?"

He lost out at GenStaff. They took his command away from him. They've handed the whole show over to bloody General Ananias.

"Including control of the spacefleet?"

Ananias has got the whole lot. He's now Senior Advisor to the General Staff.

"Where's Ananias now?"

Still out on the Intelligence radio ship, I guess. At least he's still interceptin' our transfer link to Antares.

"Which means he could be on-line?"

Correct, little soldier. Ananias's voice came in muffled but intelligible. *Glad to see you're coming back on form. That was a piece of destruction that surpassed even your demoniac best. Trouble is, you hit at the wrong side. With you around we don't need any enemies.*

"Spool the noise, Ananias. You've got to stop the Commando space-fleet before they meet the Destroyers. Cana's fleet is battle-ready and desperate. I think they'd cut the Commandos to pieces."

Relax, Bron. Those two fleets won't get within parsecs of each other. I've already taken care of that. But my real worry is you. You've not only forgotten that there was a plan—you've even forgotten that it was your plan! Don't you remember anything?

"Bits and pieces come back when I get a thread of connecting circumstances—but the overall picture escapes me."

Then, for your information, we two were up to our necks in a plot about a kilometer thick that could have gotten us hanged a dozen times had it gone wrong. The fact that we've not yet been hanged has been due almost entirely to some very fast talking on my part. But I can't keep carrying you—nobody has a fund of luck that great. You've

178

got to get yourself straightened out—and fast. In the meantime, don't make any major decisions without referring them to me. If you pull another crazy stunt like the last one we'll likely lose Terra as a result. Jaycee, are you there?

On-line, Ananias.

Look after this prize idiot. We're taking the radio ship into subspace and we won't be able to maintain our interception of the transfer link. If Bron moves out of line again clobber him with every correction circuit on the board. I'll call you again as soon as we clear the jump.

Engaged, Ananias. You must be feelin' very proud of yourself, you Godlostmewling. GenStaff has just confirmed their emergency decision. It seems that from this moment we're all workin' for you.

Have I ever told you otherwise, honey-bitch? Didn't I always tell you to be nicer to the boss? But don't let circumstances fool you. I could never have cooked up a scheme half as big and twisted as this has turned out to be. The real insane architect of our misfortunes is on the other end of this transfer link. If he hadn't so conveniently lost his memory, he'd tell you so himself.

A sudden alteration came in the quality of sound as Ananias cut his circuits out of the transmission. The difference made Bron more conscious of the background noises that entered his brain along with the hiss of the transfer-link carrier. He was alarmingly aware now of the increased strength of the goose-mutter. Not only was it greater in volume—it was also more menacing in texture. The previous babble of sounds was separating into discrete components, like the tones of individual geese talking through molasses. But whatever the language and whatever the nature of the creatures who uttered them, the urgent tones of overriding panic were implicit in the sound.

The rhythmic tones of this alien invasion into his head broke like waves on a seashore—but the waves were of waterglass and the creatures who generated them were drowning in a tide that swept shores far beyond the vast resources of the human Id. He realized with horror that if this emergent sound continued to increase in volume, there must soon come a time when it would swamp the human messages over the transfer link and leave him isolated in a gulf of foaming, gelatinous babble. In order to rescue himself from these dark concerns Bron had to force himself to concentrate on his own circumstances.

"Jaycee, is Ander still available?"

On call, Bron. Do you want me to signal him?

"Urgently. I must know what a chaos catalyst is."

Engaged, Bron. It may take a few minutes to find him. By the way, I suppose I ought to feel sorry for the way I handed you that punishment. It was intended to make you toe the line—but I guess when you're involved as we are with each other it's almost impossible to keep your own feelin's out.

"That moment was inevitable, Jaycee, wasn't it? It had to come. Do you ever think much about our relationship?"

*It's not an experience I'm likely to be forgettin',
if that's what you mean.*

"Ignoring the innuendo, that was roughly what I
meant. It reminds me of the rapport—the mysteri-
ous marriage of minds between torturer and tortured. You're more with me—and more one with
me—than would be possible in any love-love-
coupling. I sometimes even think you know what
I'm thinking."

*I frequently do. Partly instinctively and partly
because you unconsciously subvocalize a great
deal of your thinkin'. You don't transmit the
thoughts too clearly, but I can often pick up the
emotion. You don't know how I crawl when you
touch other women and I can read the conflicts in
your mind.*

"Crawl, Jaycee? And what other women? I
haven't seen one this trip."

*They're part of what you've forgotten. And
crawl is the word I mean, damn you. When your
self-pity and self-hate burst out and sour the love
and the tenderness you should have for a woman, I
feel I want to scream. I want to tell her—tell them
all—that if they understood you as I understand
you none of us would get hurt—not them and not
me.*

"Or me?"

*That isn't implicit in the relationship, Bron.
You're the sufferer and the cause of the sufferin'.
That's your role. I don't care how much you suffer
as long as our liaison's allowed to continue. I know
I'm goin' to suffer through you regardless—and
that's the fact that tells me how deeply I'm in-*

*volved. Only sometimes the rapport isn't suffi-
cient. I feel the urge to get my nails and teeth into
your flesh to even up the score. I get—high—Oh,
God! That's your type of chaos, Bron. Right across
the universe you seem to reach out and etch bits
off me.*

She broke off as if interrupted. After a short
period she came back again.

*I've got Ander on-line, Bron. I'm leavin' him
with you. Doc's takin' over the board, so if you
want anythin' further he'll be available. I'm goin'
out to get pickled so high I'll probably make orbit.*

Another voice broke in on the transfer link.
*Ander speaking. You want to know about chaos
catalysts?*

"Yes, Ander. I keep being told I am one."

*It's a fairly simple concept, Bron. You remember
we established that increases or decreases in the
normal rate of entropy were mainly the result of
intervention by some form of intelligence such as
Man's. Most individuals live their lives with very
little effect on the overall pattern of entropy and
therefore are not distinguishable singly. But there
are a few whose influence catalyzes whole
societies into new modes of action. The effective
points of their lives can be traced with some precision by entropic analysis. They cause detectable
chaos ripples as their activities alter the slope of
entropic rise or depression. We call these individuals chaos catalysts.*

"What sort of individuals are they?"

*Most of the tyrants of history—and a few of the
saints. A lot of fundamentally great thinkers,*

mainly those concerned with physical science. Almost no politicians and many, like yourself, whose innate capacity for destruction has left or will leave a permanent scar on history. The names of most of them wouldn't be familiar to you, because the judgment is based not on contemporary values but on the verified effects of the altered course of human history.

"But history has no verdict on me," objected Bron.

Not yet. But the patterns of chaos have. If we read them forward into time we can read the violence of the effects of which you will one day be the cause. It was the intensity of your chaos effects that caused the destruction of Onaris.

"That's a bit far-fetched, isn't it, Ander?"

Unhappily, no. All those millions of years ago some intelligent life form must have read the same things in the chaos patterns and been afraid. They could have had no means of knowing what was to be the origin of those ripples, but they plotted the position in space and time so accurately that the Onaris hellburner was correct within meters and only a little late in time.

"But why pick on me?"

I suspect they were trying to avert the consequences of something you're going to do—you and the other chaos experts Cana has been collecting. But you're the prime catalyst, the main causal focus. I don't know what sort of thing you're going to do, but the shock spheres of the resultant are the most violent ever recorded.

The clangor of the battle alarm shattered Bron's

speculation and brought the ship's crew to a condition of readiness with speed and precision. In Bron the alarm keyed half-forgotten instincts and he automatically surveyed the *Skua*'s bridge. With an increasingly professional eye he came to recognize the various conventions of Destroyer spacewar techniques and to translate them into terms he could understand. Then he stopped, perplexed. Instinctively his eyes had gone toward the detectors and screens that should logically be the sources of warning of approaching danger.

But the screens were blank. Not one of them held a signal that could be interpreted as the cause of a battle alarm. Likewise the detectors, while straining to search the far recesses of the void, gave no clear voice to the suggestion of approaching trouble. The eyes of the crew were intent on the computer bank, whose digital signals were trimming and correcting the detection instruments as if anticipating some nemesis as yet well below the threshold limits of the apparatus.

The situation reminded Bron of the hiatus before the Onaris hellburner had come into detection range. Here was the same atmosphere of awe and expectancy—a situation that began in anticipation.

"Doc, are you there?"

On-line, Bron.

"Make sure all the recorders are in trim. Something critical is coming up."

Engaged. By the way, do you want to give me any explanations before I have to turn my records over to the Commando Provost?

"I don't read you, Doc. What sort of charge could the Provost lay against me?"

If it's in the Criminal Indices, it'll be in the indictment.

"Try a specific summary. I haven't got much time."

Specifically, suppression of intelligence data, falsification of intelligence reports, manipulating Commando funds to finance unauthorized projects and various charges of espionage, sabotage and treason.

"That's enough to be going on with. I don't remember a damn thing about any of those, so I can't argue. How do you fit into all this, Doc?"

I'm a very disappointed man. I've worked five years with you on this project, Bron—five years that have taken more out of me than I had to give. And what do I find? You and Ananias have been using me. Playing me for a fool.

"You're no fool, Doc, and I'm sure I never took you for one. There's a good reason behind all this—only I can't quite figure it for the moment."

Then I suggest you ask Ananias, because Commando Central is gunning for him as well.

"I thought Ananias was currently on top."

Politically, yes. But legally the Commando Provost's building a case against both of you that even Ananias's patrons on the General Staff won't be able to quash. I've tried to help you, but there's nothing I can do unless you can give me an assist.

"I can't, Doc. I would if I could. But stay on-line, because some of the answers are out here and one of them could be the thing just coming up."

While he had been speaking, the detectors had increasingly tightened their positions in response to the computer's prognostication. Bron realized then, in the absence of any electronic returns by the instruments, that the current state of emergency had to be based entirely on real-time chaos predictions. The complex and diminutive ripples of the entropic waves provided the point on which the instruments were being aligned.

Gradually the screens began to display a slight electronic fuzz at the outer limits of their detection capability and well outside attack range. With some dismay he noted that the Weapons Control group did not appear to be following the hardening settings. To check this he started across the deck.

A hand arrested him. He turned to face Cana, who had come behind him unnoticed.

"I can guess what you're thinking, Syncretist—but it won't work. Chaos predicts the alien vessel within firm plotting range inside ten minutes. It also predicts that we're going to lose a ship. As soon as we can locate the alien accurately enough we'll open fire on it. But we won't alter the outcome—because we're reading the chaos resultant of an event which *has* to take place. As far as the patterns of chaos are concerned, the loss of one of our ships is already a matter of historical fact."

"Not to me it isn't," said Bron. "You'll soon have the alien's approach plotted in three dimensions plus the time component, with all the accuracy you need to make a kill. Are you trying to tell me that you can't put sufficiently heavy weapons down that line to destroy anything that has space capability?"

"Of course we can try," said Cana. "But you still haven't grasped the essential fact. We know our weaponry will not be effective, because we already know what the result will be. You can't alter a future event for which you can read the firm resultant."

"Why not?" asked Bron.

"Because to alter the unalterable is a contradiction in terms. By definition, you're defeated before you can begin to compose your defense. How can you hope to win a battle which future history has already determined you've lost?"

"I can see the argument, but I don't accept it. I don't see how the paradox could resolve itself —but that's chaos's problem, not mine."

Cana looked at Bron searchingly, then turned with swift decision. "Weaponsmaster, the Syncretist will direct the battle. Take his instructions as though they were mine."

Bron needed no second bidding. With long experience of Commando spacewar behind his intuition, he moved swiftly into action, briefing the Weapons Control crew to secure an immediate lock on the chaos coordinates. Then he turned back to Cana. "I presume you have chaos analysts who determine which patterns the computer is to process. I need to speak to them."

Cana signaled a communications man, who handed Bron a handset.

"Chaos complex on-line."

"Fine! Correct me if I'm wrong, but we're nearing a chaos resultant which appears to indicate the destruction of a Destroyer ship by alien fire."

"Da's correct."

"What in the chaos evidence leads you to infer that the resultant is, in fact, the destruction of a Destroyer ship?"

"Damn sure is ship. Eighteen teramegaton explosion don' happen in empty space unless ship and powerplant blow. Space-time coordinates indicate the corvette *Anne Marie* as only possible target approachin' that poin'. We already issued evacuation instructions for the crew."

"Then cancel them. I want the *Anne Marie* powered and headed out of the area before the resultant comes to term."

"You can' do that!" the voice was aghast. "You can' beat chaos!"

Bron turned back to Cana. "Confirm that order for me, will you? I've got something else to arrange."

He turned back to Weapons Control, began a rapid interrogation. The results were negative. He called the communications man to a conference and outlined his plan swiftly. In the face of his logic, nobody argued. In less than a minute they all knew what had to be arranged. Bron's radical approach begat an attitude of enthusiasm both infectious and in direct contrast with the former air of fatalistic acceptance. Only Cana remained unconvinced, but he did not interfere.

By now the alien vessel was clear on the screens. By human standards it was a monstrosity—an unfinished bulk of black and sinister metal, blunt, rodlike and uninspired. Although it was moving at below light speed, its velocity was still greater than that of the *Skua* and her sisters. At this distance the alien appeared eyeless and utterly without the finesse required of a vessel with deep-space capability. As the battle-computer verified its position, the alien's image steadied under the crossed hairs of the screen and the final lock-on of instruments went to completion. The Weapons Control crew was now fully attentive to the task of adjusting the last few decimal places for a detailed fix, which was at the extreme end of their weapon range.

The weaponsmaster, taking post at the communications set, talking rapidly to his opposites in other Destroyer vessels, half-turned to watch the coordinates race across the computer's readout panel. The agreement came swiftly. All positions were set and maintained on lock by the battle computer. There would be no opportunity to rethink tactics if the experiment failed. Bron watched the critical registers run toward zero and nodded his acceptance.

Human fingers keyed off the safety devices and the conduct of the battle passed into electronic hands whose reactions were limited in speed by the velocity of light alone. But nobody on the bridge was deceived about the real nature of the confrontation.

This was Bron the Syncretist against the inexorable patterns of chaos.

XV

"DID YOU SEE that ship, Doc?"

All the way, Bron. Alien as they come. No Cana trickery there. And that raises a whole load of questions. The Terran government has always denied the possibility of an alien menace and especially the possibility of alien life forms crossing the void. The last election was fought on the strength of that promise. Seems they're wrong on both counts.

"And Cana was right. The Onaris hellburner was obviously out of the same stable. It was the aliens who destroyed Onaris. And if Cana was innocent of that, how sure are we of his part in the destruction of the other planets credited to him?"

You ought to know, Bron. It was mainly you and Ananias who built up the case against the Destroyers. I'm transmitting these tapes to GenStaff. The Defense Council's going to have to do some radical rethinking in the face of this evidence. I'm recalling Jaycee to the board, but I'll stay on-line until she comes.

"Engaged." Bron watched the screens critically as the detectors cautioned that the alien ship was closing to target range. He was possessed by an unexplainable sense of something wrong, but was initially unable to place it. Then he realized that the goose-mutter in his head had died to a quiet hiss. This was not a mere attenuation of the signal—the fidelity was better than ever—but the noise was subdued, held a suggestion of hushed expectancy, as if its alien originators were also spectators of the incident about to take place.

Then, from the *Skua*'s mighty projectors, the long, slim tubes of the space torpedoes carrying diffract-meson warheads slid silently into the soundlessness of space on an intercept course. So accurate was the plotting that each would find its appointed place on the target within meters. Such accuracy was unnecessary, since a diffract-meson missile could destroy any known vessel with space capability if detonated within fifty kilometers of its target—but Bron had opted to take not even the slightest chance. Such was the range of the screens that the bright needles indicating the torpedoes appeared to move like snails toward the alien, though in reality their velocity approximated one-hundredth of the speed of light. As yet the alien showed no sign of putting up a defensive screen against the attack or of taking any evasive action.

Shortly a second salvo of missiles left the *Skua*'s projectors. These were heavy power mines of more conventional nuclear design. Their direction was not toward the alien but to the theoretical point in space where chaos had declared an explosion must soon take place. Nor was the *Skua* alone in this action. Seven other Destroyer craft were also contributing a complement of high-powered explosives to converge on this same point. Of all the ships in the neighborhood, the dark alien alone issued no fire and gave no sign of anticipated combat. It carved its way solidly through space as if no battle existed. The goose-mutter became inaudible.

The torpedoes reached their target first. The fantastic flare of the dozen diffract-meson reactions overloaded the scanners and dropped the screens into a blankness that lasted many seconds. When the screens came back to life again, gasps of dismay came from watchers on the bridge. The alien vessel was both undestroyed and apparently undisturbed. It continued to plough a steady course into the middle of the Destroyer fleet, having survived a particulate reaction calculated to annihilate completely any object made of any material found in the known universe.

A few moments later the power mines converged in space to form the eighteen tetra-megaton explosion at the empty point where chaos analysis had predicted the *Anne Marie* should have been but for Bron's intervention. The corvette itself had been hastily diverted and now lay witnessing the harmless diversion of its own fate. The explosion formed the entropic resultant required to justify the existence of the particular chaos wavefront and effectively substituted for the ship Bron had saved.

Cana's eyes were alive with speculation.

"Thank you, Syncretist! You begin to reveal a little of your promise. No other man in history has ever managed to manipulate a chaos resultant successfully. You didn't learn that trick in any mad seminary on Onaris—and I doubt it's standard Commando practice, either. You're not only a born catalyst but also a very remarkable man."

Bron's reply was halted by a sudden cry from the operator at the screens. He turned. The image of the alien ship was being held in full focus and magnified to fill the limits of the frame. Although the diffract-meson impacts had done no obvious damage, they had apparently thrown the vessel out of its bald trajectory. Now the monstrous creation was rolling and tumbling, not so much in the manner of a ship thrown out of control as like a stick thrown idly into a wind.

Bron and the Destroyers watched in fascination as the uncouth and mammoth cylinder rolled slowly end over end. They were treated to a good view of its imprecision as a ship, but gained no idea at all of its purpose or its mode of function. Then a shocking fact revealed itself. As the vessel turned it became apparent that its rear end was either missing or else had never existed. There were no drive tubes, no reaction mechanisms, no continuation even of an end wall. The whole vast structure was no more than an empty shell, a cylinder closed at one end and open to space at the other. It had no contents and no internal partitions. What form of mystery had accelerated it to such a velocity while holding it true along its major axis was a question Bron felt totally incapable of answering.

The drama deepened as he watched incredulously. The tumbling enigma passed centrally through the point where the substitute explosion had occurred and continued blindly onward. The screens adjusted suddenly past it, as if seeking foreknowledge of its destination. The graticule settled on the distant image of another corvette, the *Jubal*. Barely had the gain been adjusted to produce a reasonable image when the dark, alien cylinder hit the *Jubal* like a throwing-stick striking a bird in flight.

The conclusion was even less anticipated. By some unholy reaction both the *Jubal* and the alien artifact broke up—not apparently through force, but through a kind of mutual disintegration. There was no explosion, no obvious release of energy, merely a crazy annihilation of the mass of both bodies as they came into physical contact. Incredibly, each seemed to contain a state of matter that was the antithesis of the other. The effect was a kind of cancellation of the existence of both, with no manifestation of the latent energy that should have been the consequence of the complete destruction of so much mass. Shortly the only evidence of the event was a small quantity of space flotsam and an enigmatic question mark in the minds of the men who had observed it.

Almost immediately the goose-mutter rose to a crescendo inside Bron's head. Automatically he thought of it as the cheering of a vast crowd, yet the unintelligible semantic undertones were more indicative of fear than jubilation. However, the aliens were certainly witnesses to the event, because the timing of their resurgence was too precise to be coincidental. His mind tried to contain their alienness, but balked at the task. These creatures were things with means and talents beyond the ken of anything in human experience. He had no inbuilt references on which to hang his hazy concepts of them. Only two things they seemed to share with human kind—hostility and fear.

Cana said, "We seem to have worthy enemies, Syncretist. They're taking you on at your own game."

"How do you mean?" asked Bron.

"You cheated chaos by substituting your own reason for the existence of a wave in the pattern. They countered by destroying the *Jubal* by means that would not produce an entropic wave. By chaos analysis your method is indistinguishable from a real event, theirs, from a classic non-event. Which means we stand a very good chance of winning."

"How do you compute that?"

Cana smiled tiredly. "My dear Syncretist, we

have evidence, such as the Onaris hellburner, that the aliens have been experimenting with chaos for hundreds of millions of years. I was watching you just now and your reactions were instinctive. You evolved an answer comparable with theirs in something under seven minutes. Now I see why they're so afraid of you."

A furious burst of static in his head warned Bron of something occurring on the transfer link. Then a muffled but recognizable voice broke in.

Ananias on-line. Do you read me, honey-bitch?

Veeder reading you, Ananias. What the hell's going on?

Listen in, Doc, and keep a line open to GenStaff. I've already sent in my report. This next session's going to be critical. Bron, are you reading me?

"Like a book, Ananias. What's the readout?"

We've just cleared subspace and made rendezvous with the Commando fleet on the Rim. I've a task force of sixty-eight ships here, all battle-ready and eager for a killing. I'm broadcasting on FTL radio as well as on the transfer link because I want Cana to hear what I have to say.

"I hope you're not thinking of threatening him. He's easily got twice the firepower you can muster."

Threaten him? You must be out of your tiny addled mind. We haven't come to threaten—we've come to join him. Chaos predicts the main alien spacefleet only a few days out in the void. From the looks it's a bloody armada rather than a fleet—and it's going to do a hell of a lot of damage.

Bron turned to Cana. ''General Ananias is trying to contact you on FTL transmissions. He
reckons the alien main fleet is only a few days out
and he wants to bring the Commando fleet to
help.''

''Tell him I'll talk to him,'' said Cana. ''I'd been
wondering if he ever would keep the pact we made
on the *Tantalus* after we rescued him from the
void.''

XVI

In the *Skua*'s communications room Bron supervised the adjustment of the FTL communications web until two-way contact was established with Ananias. Cana waited impatiently until he could speak the first word.

"General Ananias—my intelligence network gives me no favorable impression of your attitude toward the so-called Destroyer federation of planets."

"I warned you at our last meeting, Cana, that such a situation might be necessary."

"Indeed yes. But for the benefit of the Commando authorities who may have access to this conversation, I should prefer to hear the record set out plainly."

"As you wish. You know as well as I that the alien menace is a real and active threat not only to the Rim Dependencies, but to your federation—and ultimately to Terra itself. We've both known this for many years. Unfortunately, such has been the insecure structure of Terran governments over that period that any account of alien threats to our galaxy has been rejected as irresponsible alarmism. The Terran standpoint is untenable. I have been in the void in command of the *Tantalus* and have personally witnessed the sort of physical threat posed by the aliens. You yourself must know only too well what type of danger they are to our existence. I think you'll agree the evidence shows they appear to have no intention of allowing humans any sort of foothold in space."

"I agree with your summary this far, General. But you dodge the issue. Why have you so persistently vilified the Destroyer nations?"

"I'm not dodging the issue. I'm attempting to explain. Since I was unable to convince the Terran government about the alien threat I had to adopt a more extreme tactic. It was obviously necessary for Terra's defense that a strong space-fleet be developed and maintained. In connivance with Commander Bron of Stellar Commando Intelligence, we deliberately attributed facets of the alien's long-range attacks to the Destroyers. By this ruse we were able to encourage Terra to invest in a superior defensive spacefleet on the misguided assumption that the Destroyers were the real enemy. Neither Bron nor myself ever believed this, but we consistently misreported the evidence to make it appear to be the truth. For some reason you were a credible danger, while the aliens were not. Since Bron is now in your hands I must make it clear that he was the major architect of our policy of deception. He is also one of the most powerful chaos catalysts our analysts have ever detected. For this reason we decided to manipulate him into the situation with the greatest concentration of firepower. That's why you now find him in your camp rather than ours.''

"Is this true, Syncretist?" asked Cana.

"I wouldn't know," said Bron. "But it does supply a lot of missing pieces. Did you say I planned this, Ananias?"

"Every crooked move of it, Bron. It was a scheme that suited your talent for playing the system against itself. You tricked the Commandos into sending you right into the hands of the Destroyers—which was where you most wanted to be. Only a few of us knew that you went to join the Destroyers rather than fight them. The trouble was, you nearly undid all of us when you lost your memory halfway through the act.''

"Accepting that, General," said Cana, "what proposition had you in mind?"

"With the evidence of this transfer-link conversation added to my own reports, Terra can no longer deny that the alien threat exists. Whether she likes it or not, Terra is now committed to help you against the common enemy. But however close the cooperation, I can't see Terra permitting her fleets to come under Destroyer control.''

''Do they need to?'' asked Cana.

''Come!'' reproached Ananias. ''You know the inverse square law as applied to spacewar battle tactics. Two small independent fleets have only a twenty-five percent chance of survival compared with one larger coordinated fleet.''

''That's statistically correct, but it still raises an impasse. Since we were lately enemies I can't happily subscribe to the notion of the Destroyer fleet becoming subject to Terran control.''

''Then here's my proposition. If I can swing Terran opinion, would you be prepared for both fleets to come under Bron? He's an experienced battle commander. He's certainly the prime chaos catalyst at this time—and his location with your fleet seems to be an effective compromise between Terran and Destroyer viewpoints.''

Cana looked at Bron speculatively. ''I've lost Martin Daiquist, my lieutenant, so I don't have a candidate of my own to offer. Having seen Bron in action just now, I'm prepared to believe that he's the one man who can handle the job. I can accept your proposition only if both fleets are subject entirely to his control—and without his being subject to pressure from Terran sources.''

Jaycee on-line, Bron. Jaycee's voice came into Bron's head alone and was not repeated over the speakers. *We've rerouted the transfer link so as not to interfere with Ananias's broadcast. GenStaff's been monitoring your conversation on-line, and they're in agreement with Ananias's scheme, if you want to follow through. The final decision's up to you.*

"That was quick, Jaycee. What shook them up?" Bron spoke subvocally.

Partly the tapes Doc took from your earlier report and partly the fact that fourteen planets of the Rim Dependencies have stopped transmitting. Three of them got out messages saying they were being attacked by something from the void. They were certain it was not the Destroyers. There was a major defense panic until somebody realized that you and Ananias already had the situation solved. Are you going to take the job?

"It's not the decision, it's the capability that worries me. Yes, I'll take it—but get hold of Ander and put him to checking through the tapes on the encounter with that alien ship-thing. There may be chaos implications there that we've missed. Certainly unless our weaponry is more effective than it was then, we're lost before we start."

Engaged, Bron. I'll be reportin' as soon as we get some answers.

Bron turned back to Cana, who had been watching the progress of the unheard conversation as it was mirrored on Bron's face.

"I have Terran GenStaff's agreement to your terms. I'll take the job on the assurance that I won't be subjected to pressures fom you either."

"You have my word on it," said Cana.

"I warn you," said Bron, "it'll be a rough ride. A little while ago you lost a perfectly good corvette to a sort of alien throw-away container. If we can't get the better of a garbage can by using diffract-meson warheads, then what the hell do you think is going to happen when we meet their battle fleet?''

"I don't know," said Cana heavily. "I've been living with that specter for years. Because of it I forged the independent planets into the Destroyer Federation, knowing all the time that we never really stood a chance if the aliens crossed the void in force. But I'm growing older and it's going to be a war for swift brains and nimble fingers. I'd groomed Martin for the job—but he couldn't survive you. Somehow I doubt the aliens will have any better luck. There's something about you, Syncretist, that is unassailable.''

"Ananias," said Bron. "Fourteen planets of the Rim Dependencies have stopped transmitting. Presumably some of the aliens got there first. Can you send a scout formation and get some positive information? Also relay to me data on what classes of ships you have available and details of their armaments. Too, you must have some kind of chaos computing complex. I want a full hookup with Cana's chaos men. The aliens have a few hundred million years start on handling chaos and I want us to catch up fast.''

Engaged, Bron. You know, this is quite like old times—

"Then get off-line and get busy. Put a few scout-ships out in the void and try to get us some facts and figures about the strength and disposition of the alien fleet. And stay off the transfer link. Use the FTL radio unless you have an extreme emergency.''

There was the sudden cessation of the hiss of a carrier wave as Ananias cut out his circuits. Now that the bio-electronic relay had less to contend with, he was again conscious of the sound of drowning geese. Perhaps twenty individual voices predominated over the general babble and these prime spokesmen rippled across the audible spectrum in a hideously broken yodel, as though their voices were modulated by large bubbles rising through a silo of molasses. Their mood sounded nervous, quick and urgent, as if indicating that time was a critical factor of their actions.

The babble was hypnotic and he was powerless to shut it out. The rise and fall of the anxious spokesmen suggested the swell of a stygian river, while the quieter, more powerful background mutter was that of a pressing tide. Perhaps an ultrasonic ceiling to the echo in the voices gave the impression of a cavern roof, caught under hundreds of kilometers of dark pressure, yet extending onward like a dreadful pipe leading into an unknown darkness.

He had no doubt now that these were the voices of the aliens in the void. By some obscure trick of physics, their communications system infringed on his own transfer link. If their voices could fetch him such strange and alien visions, he wondered equally what the byplay between Jaycee and himself could mean to them. He was not even sure at times what it meant to him—let alone her.

XVII

"AND THAT'S THE score at the moment." Ananias's voice came wearily over the FTL radio. "An advance party of about a hundred alien vessels is already within the confines of the Milky Way. This appears to be the spearhead of the main attack force still moving in from the void."

"Didn't the advance party show up on chaos analysis?"

"Yes, but we couldn't determine the significance of our readings. Some activity was apparent in the direction of the Space Dependencies, but we couldn't plot its position accurately—we were working with too short a baseline. Now that we have access to the Destroyer chaos records we can correlate with a fair degree of accuracy.''

''Now is too late,'' said Bron. ''It should have been done five years ago.''

''Agreed. You and Cana and I know that, but Terra couldn't be bothered to listen. How do you want to play this, Bron?''

''We must know more about their craft and their weapons. We need to experiment with tactics on a limited scale before we're forced into contact with their main fleet. Prepare six battle cruisers to make a direct attack on the smallest grouping of alien ships you can locate.''

''Why not use the whole fleet?''

''Because any ship of ours that goes into that battle may not come out again. I want the maximum amount of information from the minimum number of ships at risk. All data on weapons effectiveness, both positive and negative, are to be transmitted via FTL radio and recorded for analysis.''

''Engaged.''

Ananias cut transmission. Bron relaxed slightly and looked along the *Skua*'s bridge, which had become his command post and had been virtually his home during the past thirty-six hours. All the communications posts were fully manned by the extrovert but nonetheless efficient Destroyer technicians. His assumption of Daiquist's former position had gone smoothly. Bron had the feeling that his somewhat unusual status as a master syncretist, plus his obvious familiarity with battle command procedure, had already created around him something of a legend. Certainly he could have asked no more in the way of respect and willing obedience from the tough Destroyer shipmen.

The *Skua* and a hastily regrouped assortment of seven Destroyer ships had left the comforting rimline of the extremities of the Milky Way and were now engaged in their own exploratory run, similar to the one being undertaken by General Ananias and the Commando fleet well within the Rim. Bron could feel the weight of a great loneliness—it beset his mind as the ship carved deeply into the terrifying void between the great galactic clusters. The eight were on the trail of a lone alien straggler, which purely random chance had detected as a solitary, isolated pinpoint in the wastes of extragalactic space.

The detectors had already located and confirmed the course of the alien and soon the screens were beginning to pull in the first indications of electronic contact. The weapons crew were busily setting up their missile programs, but Bron decided not to call for a chaos analysis of the outcome of the attack. He preferred to go into battle still full of the undimmed hope that an adverse analysis would have destroyed. The eight vessels all had a specific pattern of weapons to employ and the directive was simple—after performing the allocated task they were to withdraw out of attack range and stand by for further orders.

Soon the alien was clear upon the screens, a trimmer, more acutely wicked craft than the one that had destroyed the *Jubal*. This craft was covered with faceted nodules that might have been weapon points or merely a peculiarity of the hull plating. As he watched the critical registers run toward battle-zero, Bron again sensed the quieting of the alien tongues in his head—the hushed expectancy. The babble fell to a low moan, a tense anticipation. Anticipation of what? One does not anticipate defeat or victory with quiet expectation—only the springing of a trap!

Instantly he was on his feet and running toward the communications point, shouting with such urgency that all eyes turned to him.

"Abort the attack! All ships abort the attack and drive clear. Crash emergency!"

The image on the screens dropped out of focus as the *Skua* swung into a violent turn that almost broke her spine. The great ship fled in the tightest arch its gravitic compensators would allow it to follow without destroying the crew. Even so, a lack of compensation of several gravities subjected the men to a stress component many times that to which they were accustomed. But as the screens came back into focus, the sounds of complaint died immediately.

Bron's outburst had been justified.

The alien ship blew up. It split in one incredible

second to form a fireball that became a raging quasi-stellar inferno and finally a quasi-star. The shipboard radiation detection systems screened warnings of impending breakdown of the biological protection screens. Then the mad sun collapsed and died, its energy consumed and dissipated in its short but fantastic life.

Bron called in his companion ships. Not one had suffered serious damage. Their captains were grateful—though still bewildered by the orders that had brought them out of the maw of a searing death. Another part of the Bron legend had been added to the Destroyer chronicles.

Bron was unable to explain. He was having an increasingly difficult time hearing normal conversation above the rising level of angry goose-snarl and bicker the futile loss of the alien ship-weapon had evoked. When his head-noise finally quieted he called Commando Control.

"Are you there, Jaycee?"

On-line Bron.

"Anything to report from your end?"

They're having trouble with noise in the Antares receiver. Sounds like somethin' boilin' in a pot. They're filterin' it out now, but it was bad a short while ago. That was quite a fireworks display you just had.

"They used to serve a drink with a comparable effect in a little bar at the back of Europa Commando Base. Six shots and you woke three days later with radiation sickness instead of a hangover. I could do with a bottle right now."

Jaycee began to laugh. *Sounds like the old Bron memory might be returnin'.*

"It is, in little unconnected bits. But most of what comes back I'd as soon not remember. And I still can't remember you. Should I?"

That's classified information, Bron. I can't give you an answer.

"Damn it, I demand an answer."

You're not gettin' one. While we're coupled on a mission, we're part of a psychologically matched team. We don't dare do anythin' to upset that, Bron—if it goes out of balance the linkage becomes quite intolerable. Especially for you.

"And for you, Jaycee?"

I don't count. I have to solve my problems my own way. But you can tolerate me in your head for such long periods of time only because I supply somethin' your personality needs. You may be a warlord to Cana and the General Staff, but I know you're a Godlost louse and it's my job to make sure you never forget it.

"Thanks for nothing. But you've given me something I'm going to work on. Did you get me any answers from Ander yet?"

He's in the viewing room feeding maths into the computer terminal like he was payin' the rent out of his own pocket. Do you want him on-line?

"Not if he hasn't finished. Just add the tapes of that last alien encounter to the stuff he's already working through. Might give him something new."

Are you on to somethin', Bron?

"I have a feeling that the aliens aren't going to

be defeated by conventional weapons. If they've studied our chaos patterns over the ages, they'll know all too well the limitations of our present arms technology. If they're the master technologists they seem to be, they'll already have made sure that their fleet is relatively immune to our diffract-meson and other particulate reactions. Yet we must have acquired something that's worrying them, I believe, or they wouldn't have moved so suddenly against us at this particular time."

And you think you have a line on our worry factor?

· "All the evidence points to this—it has something to do with chaos. They tried to stop Cana from acquiring chaos men. They tried to stop me on Onaris. They used a sort of chaos non-event weapon on the *Jubal*. It begins to look as if chaos itself holds the key to the battle. But how to fight a physical spacewar using a mathematical abstraction is something I don't begin to understand."

"Receiving you, Ananias. How did it go?"

"Diabolically, Bron. We lost all six ships to the weirdest space strategy I ever saw. The aliens rammed them."

"They what?"

"Rammed our ships in straight collision courses—in one-for-one exchanges. Whichever way our ships turned, one of those damned aliens swooped on it and exploded. I'm worried, Bron. When we battle that fleet coming in from the void, we won't have the numbers to fight them on such a basis. And our weapons don't touch them at all."

"You've met them in space before, on the *Tantalus*. Tell me about that time."

"That was different. The *Tantalus* was on a deep-space exploratory voyage. We dropped out of the subspace about nineteen parsecs out from the Rim to establish real-space bearings. To our astonishment we immediately picked up readings of a ship closeby. We know now that they must have been aliens using a chaos prediction on our drop-out point, but in those days chaos to us was scarcely more than a toy. The coincidence of another vessel's being so close to us after our casual drop-out seemed remarkable. We tried to make contact, but received no answer to our signals. Next the alien came straight at us on a crash course. There was an explosion or something— I've never quite been able to remember what— and I blacked out, probably for a long time. When I came around, the crew was dead and the whole ship seemed foreign and strange. It took me quite a while to accept that both the ship and I had undergone lateral inversion. At first I was convinced that it was purely a trick of eyesight. I don't know what killed the remainder of the crew, but it seemed to be some sort of shock."

Ananias paused for Bron's reaction. Bron said nothing. Ananias went on.

"I drifted for days. I had no crew to run the ship and not much of it would have functioned in any case. It took all my effort just to stay alive, patching a life-support system onto a rather inadequate emergency supply. Finally Cana's long-range detection system must have spotted the *Tantalus*—they sent out a patrol to investigate.

"Cana wanted the warning about the reality of the aliens conveyed to Terra in no uncertain terms. I agreed to take back his message. He had me put on a tramp ship at the freeport on Stere and I returned to Terra and told the story straight. It was interpreted as an elaborate lie to save my skin—with the suggestion that I'd sold the *Tantalus* to the Destroyers. I was officially reprimanded—but unofficially I had a few friends who took the warning seriously. One of them was you—"

"All right—we'll go into that later. First let's see if we can wring some sense out of what we know about the aliens thus far," Bron cut in. "We've already seen them use four different modes of destructive or disruptive space attack—the non-event destruction of the *Jubal*, the ramming of your six ships, the explosive destruction of the one I attacked, and the lateral-inversion shock on the *Tantalus*. None of those modes involved weapons as such—the aliens may not have evolved any. They appear to rely on the use of their ships, kamikaze fashion, as destructive instruments. But all these modes involve materials and methods that belong to an order of science well beyond our present grasp of physics. Additionally, all four are completely different. Since the incidents were well separated in time and space it seems reasonable to suppose that we haven't yet seen the full spectrum of the enemy's destructive effects."

"Would they employ variation for variation's sake?" asked Ananias. "Or do you suspect some other significance?"

"I suspect deeper significance. They've spent millions of years experimenting with chaos analysis. I've already proved that if you can provide an effective substitute for a predicted event—you can cheat the chaos prediction. But there's a limit to the range of substitute effects we can manufacture. I think they've analyzed this coming battle many times over and stacked the deck heavily in their favor, knowing we can't match them on their tactics. We don't have enough ships."

"Which means we're damned from the start."

"Not necessarily. There's a logical consequence to that line of reasoning that may be the piece missing from the puzzle."

"I'm damned if I can see it," said Ananias. "But then I seldom could follow the deviations of your tortuous mind."

"Look at it this way, Ananias. Suppose you were playing a computerized war game. Having taken a sound theoretical beating, you would reconsider your tactics, evolve a new strategy, and submit your revised program for a re-run. Given enough imagination and sufficient computer time, you could ultimately evolve a technique that predicted a high probability of victory against any odds."

"Agreed. But I don't see how it applies in this case."

"Suppose the aliens played a war game on the coming battle, using chaos to analyze the results. Suppose they saw they would lose it, went back and tailored the embryo designs of their fleet. Then they re-ran and kept tailoring until they thought they had the right answers. Don't you see the logical inference?"

"Frankly, no."

"Then I'll tell you. It means that chaos predictions are not fixed and immutable. There must be parallel alternate tracks where the final resultant is dependent on some branching in the chain of causality. There are actual decision points that can change the entire structure of future history. Perhaps that's the role of a chaos catalyst. Perhaps he alone can break the predetermined web and shift the future to a new track."

"My God, Bron! If you're right—"

"I have to be right, Ananias, because if I'm wrong there won't be much hope for Homo sapiens when that armada gets through."

"How do you plan to make use of the idea?"

"By inserting some of the Bron brand of chaos into the general situation to give us time to breathe. I want to try playing the system against itself. You've got a transfer link transceiver in your radioship?"

"Yes, but I don't see—"

"Hook up the receiver to your most powerful FTL radio transmitters and have all ships lock on to that. On the transfer link you'll find an alien signal. Antares is having trouble with it, so you must be able to receive it. When you're approaching a battle situation during which the aliens get tense, you'll find the signal quiets down. When they sound hushed and expectant—worried— that's the time to get out fast.''

''How will that help?''

''Past performance tends to indicate that a percentage of the aliens will destroy themselves at that critical point. We can avoid some of the disasters by making use of this real-time feedback on when to quit. They'll probably catch on to the tactic soon enough—but I think we'll have them worried for a while—''

The clangor of the battle alarm tore Bron from the handset and sent him racing for the screens. As yet nothing was visible, but the computer output terminal was angry with coordinates and course predictions of ships that seemed to occupy a mammoth arc in space. To judge from the activity, many hundreds of alien ships were approaching from the void. A large number of them were exhibiting chaos shockfronts that foretold of ultra-violent entropic changes.

Bron had a sudden change of mind. He ran from the bridge to the ship's chaos complex, calling for a forward scan of the patterns containing the *Skua*'s own red shipline trace. The computation was hastily set and the long graph of chaos ripples that surrounded the ship's existence began to issue from the plotter. For a sweep extending several hours ahead, the red trace ran unwaveringly down the center of the chart, showing no deviations despite the turbulence of the patterns in the near continuum. Then, at a particular point, the red trace leaped to a maximum—and fled immediately to zero.

A startled murmur rose from the assembled technicians as the prediction of the end of their own existence was registered only a few hours away in time. Bron cut in curtly.

"Run that scan again to the same point. As soon as you reach the falloff, reset and start again. Let me know as soon as you obtain a difference between two consecutive scans."

He became aware that Cana had entered the complex and was taking an acute interest in the proceedings.

"What are you up to, Syncretist? Are you still trying to prove that the future doesn't necessarily have to happen?"

"I submit there's a flaw in chaos theory and I'm determined to prove it."

"With all those alien ships coming in you'll need a miracle more than a theory. You have about four hours to disprove the tenets of a complete science."

"Chaos is neither complete nor science," said Bron. "Think about it. The aliens wouldn't have tried to stop me on Onaris if they had seriously believed I was going to fall four hours from this moment.

Back on the bridge the screens were now showing myriad points of unresolved lights—the alien armada was crowding in from the void. A chill tension governed the actions of the crew—even with the Commando fleet to back them, the defenders were hopelessly outnumbered. The further knowledge that they had no effective weapons superimposed on the tension a sort of dumb fatalism quieter than panic and strangely, not entirely devoid of hope.

"Jaycee, get me Ander. Urgent."

I've got him on-line, Bron. I thought you'd need him around now.

"Good girl. Ander—I suspect there's a flaw in chaos theory. I'm suggesting that a future event established by chaos analysis doesn't necessarily have to happen. I submit that cause and effect may be made to diverge and that the initially recorded resultant may not in fact be the final one."

It's part of Yohann's multi-field theory. The idea is well supported by mathematics but has never been verified.

"I think I may have that verification. You've been going through the tapes, so you'll recall I cheated chaos a little by arranging a substitute explosion in lieu of the destruction of the *Anne Marie*. Was that not a divergence of the causal chain?"

Only a slight deviation. Another ship, the Jubal, *was destroyed instead.*

"Yes, but destroyed at a later point in time. What if in that borrowed time something in the situation had given rise to a new chain of causality? The new chain could not have existed had not the original one diverged."

A brilliant bit of theorizing, Bron. But there's no

proof. Unfortunately nothing happened to initiate a new chain in that borrowed time.

"Oh, but it did, Ander. In that time I made the decision to ask you to check the tapes of the incident, and a direct consequence of my having done so is this present conversation—and any actions I may take because of it. If the original chain had not diverged, this particular conversation could never have occurred."

A silence ensued while Ander thought the situation through.

Point conceded, Bron! The full implications are too big to be swallowed at one gulp, but I would say you have produced valid proof of a deliberate redirection of history.

"That's all I wanted to know," said Bron. "I'm going to play that angle, if necessary, until the universe breaks up."

He broke off as an excited chaos technician came up, waving a chartstrip at him.

"She impossible, but 'ave 'appened. Shipline does no' go zero any more. Is what you call bloody magic! Is insane!"

"Insane or not," said Bron, "it's the way things are going to be from now on. From now on I'm taking a hand in deciding what the resultant's going to be. But I'll tell you one thing, I doubt the universe will ever be the same again."

You're not only a Godlost louse, you're a Godlost egotistical louse. Jaycee said bitchily deep inside his head. *Cut loose like that again and I'll tell you things about your mother that will make you wish you'd been born from an egg-case.*

XVIII

"Ananias, did you get that alien signal on FTL transmission yet?"

"About two minutes ago, Bron. We're currently raising a radio alert to make sure all fleetships lock on to the transmission and relay it for the captain's attention."

"Good. Make sure the captains know how to use it. I've ordered the Destroyer fleet to lock on to the same frequency. Since there's only one signal, we'd better try to phase our attacks so that we don't have two in progress simultaneously. I'm gambling on the fact that the aliens may not have FTL radio—so they won't suspect how they're being anticipated. Use normal weaponry during the attacks in order to disguise our change of tactics.''

''Engaged, Bron. Do you want us to move straight in?''

''As soon as you're ready. We're just mustering formation. Then we're going to move straight down the centerline and have a crack at anything that comes.''

''I'll say one thing for you,'' commented Ananias. ''When it comes to backing hunches, you back yours in a big way.''

Bron broke the connection then called Cana on the shipboard communicator. The span of alien ships now swam large on the screens.

''We're set to attack in about ten minutes. I'd be happier if you'd consent to board a corvette heading out of battle range.''

''Why?'' asked Cana. ''What had you in mind?''

''We're going to try a technique that may upset the balance of chaos to a point where we can't rely on analysis for our answers. We've no means of telling whether this ship—or any ship—will survive the battle. I'd prefer to see you headed safely toward baseworld.''

''If we lose this battle,'' said Cana, ''the aliens will come straight through anyway. There won't be any baseworld to be safe on. Thank you, but I'll stay aboard the *Skua*.''

''As you wish. I merely thought I'd let you know the odds.''

"Bron, in the short time I've known you I've lost every certainty I ever had about life and the nature of the universe. You don't play the odds— you bend them to fit the way you want to go. You're one of the most terrifying characters I've ever met."

I'll second that! said Jaycee archly.

Lightly at first, then with an increasingly sonorous thunder, the mighty gravitic drives bit into the fabric of space and hurled their charges toward the alien horde. Ahead of the great ships, like a miniature fleet in itself, drove a wave of diffract-meson torpedoes, potential miniature novae running like avid hounds before a hunt. The images on the screens lost their multiplicity and began to concentrate on narrower, more detailed fields as the Destroyer fleet flung itself straight at the unknown enemy.

A chorus of alien voices rose in a complex wave inside Bron's head—he detected patterns of rising alarm, of jubilation, of expectancy and fear. The speaker at his elbow repeated the diversity of sounds—but though he had control of the speaker's volume, he had no such power to protect himself from the sounds within him.

Then came the first contact. The abortive flare of diffract-meson warheads hazed the screens momentarily. When they cleared again it was to reveal three Destroyer ships concentrating on an alien pacemaker. The ships dived in a perfectly conventional attack maneuver and the alien signal fell to a hushed moan. At its ultimate atonal expression of expectancy the Destroyer ships pulled clear. For an instant nothing happened—then the alien was engulfed by a flame that stripped its very atoms of cohesion and scattered an impossible bloom of unknown ionization broadly across deep space.

In Bron's head the alien voices sang their wrath large and venomously. He was not dismayed. He had already calculated a method of keeping their complaints within a tolerable range. With sure fingers on the console keys, he signaled the next sortie.

Two Destroyer corvettes, displaying an admirable turn of speed, shot straight toward a configuration of three alien vessels on what was apparently a deliberate crash course. For once the aliens seemed to falter. Two made hasty course corrections as if to avoid the impudent aggressors. The third stuck doggedly to its route and Bron suspected that it was yet another gutted container.

With a precision beautiful to watch the corvettes bore down mercilessly upon their prey. Though Bron had planned the maneuver, even he was caught by the suspense of the action, was seized with a sudden fear that the plan had misfired. Both craft approached their targets to incredibly narrow limits before they vanished abruptly from the sky. Only the voices of their captains still reciting tachyon coordinates on the subspace radio convinced him that all had gone as intended and that the corvettes had slipped safely into the subspace continuum.

Disappointingly, the alien ships did not immediately perform their suicidal role. They clung for several seconds to their crash-evasion courses, apparently not convinced that their attackers had actually gone. One, however, had adopted a setting that took it too close to the undeviating "container" ship. They touched, and both ships broke apart with the same type of eventless energy reaction that had destroyed the *Jubal*. The trajectory of the remaining vessel took it lazily through the fringes of the crumbling flotsam before it, too, fell apart like tin held in too hot a flame.

An almost complete silence now quelled the alien voices. It was untypical, warning Bron that some new factor was entering the battle. Immediately he had a suspicion that the fight was not destined to be one-sided. Vainly he hunted across the screens, trying to identify the threat. He saw the pattern too late to figure out its portent. Seven alien ships were involved, one centrally and the rest ranged in regular array in a vast ring a half-million kilometers in diameter—which included nearly half the compass of the Destroyer fleet. Superficially nothing was different about these vessels except that they kept station in this unusual formation with completely mathematical precision.

The alien mutter fell below the audible threshold. Plainly some diabolical purpose lay behind the strange formation, whose function Bron found impossible to imagine. Unfortunately he did not have time to search for an answer. A Destroyer battle cruiser, reading no significance in the design, attempted to pass between the hub-ship and the exterior ships of the ring. The cruiser was vaporized instantly—some unknown molecular lightning had flashed between the hub-ship and one of the ring-ships. The fact that this unlikely pulse was a quarter of a million kilometers in length did not seem to attenuate its effects.

Bron winced and closed his eyes as the major disaster struck his fleet. Fully thirty Destroyer vessels, unable to identify their particular danger or unable to maneuver in time, were caught by the grisly lightning. The blazing lines of fire cut a wide core through the Destroyer ranks.

The alien expectancy noise now was up full. Above its tones Bron's orders were rapid and articulate. Ships on the fringes of the fleet were ordered to attack the alien ring-ships by approach from outside the ring's circumference. Two ships misjudged the relevant positions and were consumed. Then came a stroke of genius—a cruiser's captain put an unmanned pinnace on a crash course with a ring-ship. The alien vessel exploded in a blaze of pure energy. Unbalanced, the remaining ring-ships discharged their bolts at each other as well as at the hub-ship. The disk within the ring became a blaze of energy of a type that should never have existed outside of the structure of an atom. Bron held his head as the ring collapsed. He strove to restrain a scream as wave after wave of alien reaction threatened to swamp his reason and drive the logic from his head.

After a quarter of an hour the bitter outcry quieted. Bron began to receive reports of the cost of the operation to the Destroyer fleet. He had lost more than fifty ships and another twenty had taken precipitate jumps into subspace. A few might one day return. His confidence shaken and his forces dangerously depleted, Bron could only stare at the oncoming armada and wonder what the end was going to be.

He felt lonely and inadequate.

Don't think I'm cryin' for you, said Jaycee brutally. *I always knew you were a congenital loser. I've got Ander on-line. He's not only a man—he's got ideas.*

"I've got ideas, too. One day I'm going to beat hell out of you, Jaycee. But I could use something constructive right now. What's the readout, Ander?"

I was puzzled by that shell of a ship, Bron. I ran a chaos analysis back to its origin. It's contemporary with the Onaris hellburner—in fact the whole fleet is. They've all been in space for seven hundred million years and made the whole journey at sublight speed.

"Hell—are you sure?"

There's no doubt of it. The theory accounts for the throw-away containers. According to my calculations better than ninety-nine percent of that fleet must by now consist of gutted provision ships.

"That puts a slightly different complexion on things," said Bron. "At least I'm now only looking for a few dozen manned ships in the whole outfit."

Probably fewer than that. Anyway, you have the great psychological advantage.

"How do you compute that?"

Self-evident. Meeting you is the climactic point of some seven million centuries of endeavor. No life-form, whatever its psychology, could regard that point lightly. In fact, you're the reason the fleet exists! There's no evidence to show whether its builders are a race with exceptional longevity or whether they've bred through many generations on the journey—but either way, you're a super-legend. Would you dare to take on God Almighty?

"Frankly, I'd cringe at the thought—if I were convinced he existed."

Precisely. But they are convinced that you exist. That's why I think the raid is defensive rather than offensive.

"Defensive? You have to be joking, Ander."

Not at all. Lacking subspace access, not one of those ships can ever return. There's no point in their engaging in a destructive attack—unless it's a sort of last-ditch defense. No, Bron. This is a one-way suicide mission, hell-bent on trying to divert some aspect of chaos-predicted future history.

"If that diversion includes the destruction of the Destroyer space-force, then they're close on target. Even their empty container ships are pretty formidable weapons."

Quite deliberately, intended as such, I suspect. For that sort of journey every atom of payload would have to be worth its weight in potential. Knowing in advance the physical effects available to us, the aliens would have engineered virtually every molecule in the fleet both to withstand our destructive capability and to destroy in ways against which we'd have no defense.

"What you're postulating substantially agrees with what we're finding. Even the empty hulks are immune to particulate and nuclear reactions. Their only weak point seems a susceptibility to self-destruction initiated by near or complete contact . . . Jupiter! Ander, I think you may have given me an answer. The function of a catalyst is not to cause a reaction but to accelerate a reaction already latent. In fact, to outplay the system at its own game."

The next moments saw Bron running across the bridge, calling for the weapons master and the ship's armorer. He outlined his new tactics to them, set them moving on the double to make the necessary modifications in *Skua*'s torpedo warheads. He instructed the ship's captain to locate a suitable target for an experiment, then spent a few fleeting instants advising Jaycee of his view of her place in the lower firmament. Having done this last he felt much better.

Already the aliens apparently sensed the new excitement. The waves of muttering grew shorter in period and a spreading panic seemed to be expressing itself in a volume of sound steadily rising toward some thixotropic crescendo it never actually attained. Bron could even detect quick and urgent voices, individuals calling and responding, a nervously increasing tension that hinted of fear and anger and terrible resentment. He could almost picture the aliens crowded in darkness, dripping with moisture, smelling of unknowable fluids because of too close confinement with impossible engines. He thought he could read their leaning toward violent death as a final escape from a foredoomed and long-suffered incarceration.

His target chosen, Bron waited for the armorer's clearance on the weaponry. He did not get the go-ahead until his ship had entered battle range. There were only seconds to go before the critical registers would run to zero. Knowing that he was now committed, he keyed his confirmation and allowed the computers to take over battle-control.

With the alien target ship clear upon the screens, he watched the long slim space-torpedoes slide out. Their progress across the space vector seemed maddeningly slow. The tension rose audibly among the Destroyer crew.

As the torpedoes crawled toward their target the magnification of the screens increased to provide a close-up of the area where the actual strike would take place. Normally a strike's reaction brilliance overloaded the screens and precluded any viewing of the exact moment of impact—but when Bron's modified torpedoes hit no energy was released from the projectiles themselves. Instead, the stricken alien put out crazy spirals of some unknown mode of energy discharge. The screens remained clear.

For a tense moment the alien craft developed long, coruscating helixes of purple fire, like some surrealistic porcupine. These discrete rays of energy lengthened to peacock-tail configurations and could easily have enveloped any closely attacking ship. Then the curious emanation collapsed and died, leaving only ion-contaminated vacuum to mark the place where the ship had been. Almost the entire mass of the alien ship had been converted to controlled-release radiation—a fantastic technical potential, the purpose of which had been thwarted by Bron's modified weapon.

Throughout the entire episode the goose-mutter had been subdued and anxious. This time there was no returning roar, only a continuing murmur of despondency and fear. Bron ordered another target ship to be found, and he relayed details of the new technique to several companion ships. He sensed that somehow the aliens could read the consequences of his decision-making. The steady depression in their voices convinced him that his present course of action was going to swing the battle decisively in his favor.

A second successful sortie reinforced his conviction that he was on a winning streak. Soon two other fleetships reported enthusiastically that the method worked. The promise of again being able to attack with long-range weaponry galvanized the Destroyer fleet into action. It was for this type of spacewar that the crews had been trained and the magnificent ships equipped. Now they were again the Destroyers in a truly literal sense.

Bron winced as he saw a hundred of his ships simultaneously engage the enemy. The bronze-hued ships moved like fireflies, weaving intricately slow patterns against the vast backdrop of the void. The dark alien vessels maintained the meticulously straight, lonely courses of the damned. Soon the aliens were erupting into futile suicidal reactions in half a hundred different modes of physical disruption. Great wastes of space became momentary suns or were lit with vast tracts of impossible ionization. Sometimes these reactions were so fierce and numerous that a new galaxy seemed being born beyond the shores of the Milky Way.

"Ananias. Come in, Ananias."

"On-line, Bron. We can see you now. That looks like quite a party you're having."

"Yes. We've found their Achilles' heel. Their vessels are not susceptible to destructive reaction, but they destruct themselves if subjected to physical contact. Our normal space missiles had proximity fuses, so they never made physical contact before they actuated. All we're doing is taking the fuses out of the warheads."

"But if you withdraw the fuses, the warheads can't activate!"

"They don't need to. The entire alien fleet is on a suicide run. Every damn atom of it is programed for catastrophic destruction. All you have to do is trigger it."

Space blossomed before the *Skua* with a hundred fleeting suns. Ion trails glowed like neon bars. Red, violet and yellow fire pockets sprouted like fantastic flowers in space. An insane landscape of insubstantial radiation effects was emerging plainly on the broad canvas of nothingness. The alien voices were now a continuous scream of fear without perceptible inner-modulation or separation of components—but rapidly becoming thinner, as though the members of the unholy choir were sinking one by one and drowning in their terrible pool of fire.

XIX

FINALLY THE ALIEN voices faded and died, the last traces lingering like smoke after a summer's fire. As the Commando fleet cut through to join the Destroyers it was already apparent that Bron was going to win the battle. Soon the ships from the combined fleets simply ranged wide through space, seeking and destroying stragglers. Ultimately there was a silence in Bron's head.

He felt a compelling wave of fatigue sweep over him. He had not slept for better than thirty hours. When the trailing fringes of the battle no longer demanded his immediate attention he quit his desk, went to his bunk and fell instantly asleep.

After a while it seemed that a gentle rocking motion aroused him to a semiconscious dream state. A part of his mind realized that this was an illusion produced within sleep, yet some analytical faculty remained intrigued by the detail inherent in the recurring nightmare. Instead of rejecting the situation and forcing himself awake, he allowed himself to follow the fantasy. It started with an almost complete absence of tactile sensation, as though his mind had become insulated from his body or his body from reality. Yet he was aware of the ripple and eddy of a gentle tide that bore him over black waters.

The impression deepened until it achieved the status of reality. There was no light, but the fidelity with which the elements of the pattern came together was so consistent as to be perfectly believable. He could hear the slight wash and lap of small ripples against the tunnel walls and the quick near-ultrasonic echoes that gave proportion to the dark tunnel down which he was being drawn. Somewhere ahead a phantom goose was piping through a layer of slime with a plaintive concern that had no human associations.

A sudden bend in the impossible river made itself clearly felt as his imaginary raft fouled some jagged corner and swung him around before allowing the dark sluice to carry him on. Somewhere on his way the solitary glutinous goose was joined by another and then by an increasing number to raise a harrowing hymn that filled him with a cold horror. Another bend, and this time he clearly felt the bump against the bank . . . felt the bump . . . on his suit . . .

Suit? His shocked fingers explored, found slight seams in the inner lining of heavy gloves. His whole body confirmed the suggestion that his earlier lack of sensation had been the combined effect of his being confined in the padded recesses of an exceptionally heavy-duty spacesuit and of a numbness of the flesh, presumably from his having lain in one position overlong. These factors, plus a light gravity and the buoyancy of the fluid in which he floated face up, explained his lack of tactile sensation and his appreciation of the direction and motion of the tide. Nothing explained, though, why he was conscious of the detail of so unlikely a situation—or what diabolical things were waiting for him around those stygian bends.

The goose-mutter rose into a braying scream, a chorus of dissent, accusation, rebuke. The quality of the dreadful sound alone would have been sufficient to make him flee from the encounter had he been able to control his actions. As it was, floating on his back in a nearly unmaneuverable suit, he had no more power to resist his journey than if he had been an upturned beetle in a racing gutter stream. Hundreds of millions of years of fear and hatred were being vocally compressed into a jarring anthem of complaint and the bitterest of reproaches by something that waited for him around the final turn of the river.

Panic swamped his reason. He struggled against the encumbering suit, fretting at his inability to move his arms. Restrained and helpless, he waited with dreadful anticipation as the inexorable tide bore him around the curve. Overhead a million pressures leaned their dark depressions on the tunnel roof. The air he was breathing was hot and moist with the sweat from his fear and so tainted by metal and plastic that it soured his tongue. At any moment now he would emerge to face persecutors who had planned his murder at a time when life on Terra had still been struggling for an identity separate from the non-living elements of the primeval soup.

He had no idea of what their faces or forms would be like, but he doubted that his sanity would stand the revelation. The scolding choir was now so near that he felt he ought to be able to stretch out and touch the violent and anguished creatures. He felt there ought to be a light—but he could discern none at all. Then another voice crept in, quieter at first, but gradually pulling at him with such urgency that he had to turn toward it regardless of suit or geese or the drag of the unknown tide.

Perhaps in the sordid cells of some inhuman inquisition a spirit snapped . . .

"Jaycee, help me!"

. . . the mind mazed not by the searin' steel, the nibblin' nerve . . .

"Jaycee, for God's sake, get me out of here!"

. . . but by a vaster wound. DON'T YOU KNOW

THAT GOD IS DYIN' . . . DYIN' . . .

"Jaycee, I don't know a blessed thing about God, but get me out of this."

You're coming out, Bron. Hold on a little longer. Your metabolism is improvin' fast and your heartbeat's almost back to normal.

Bron opened his eyes. An oxygen mask was pressed across his face and beyond it the concerned eyes of a medic were watching him anxiously. As he focused his vision he found he was no longer in his bunk but on an operating table in the *Skua*'s medical bay.

"What happened, Jaycee?"

You went into a coma about seventeen hours ago. The medics tried to pull you out but were unsuccessful. Finally I had to use the semantic trigger to force you around, because your body processes were running dangerously low. I've been in contact with Ananias and we were about to authorize a heart massage.

"I had that dream again, Jaycee. The one where I'm floating in a tunnel and the aliens are waiting for me. I've got one more curve to go before I meet whatever they are—"

The aliens haven't given up yet, Bron. You've beaten their fleet, but they've established some other method of gettin' at you. Somehow they're workin' on your mind.

"Those alien signals on the transfer link. Can you still hear them?"

Stronger than ever. Antares is filterin' them out for us, but they're still comin' in.

"The alien fleet signals faded toward the end of

241

the battle. What we're getting now must be long-range stuff from the alien's point of origin. It's some sort of encoded imagery transmitted as sound. It seems to be their form of communication. I can even grasp pictures from it myself at times. But when I'm relaxed the effect can be quite hypnotic."

That computes. Your coma was consistent with the effect of ultra-deep hypnosis. That explores levels of consciousness down to about what we used for the Haltern character synthesis. It's dangerous territory to leave exposed to the use of an enemy.

"I don't feel this as an attack. I feel it's some attempt at communication."

They're just tryin' to kill you, Bron. Plain old-fashioned murder.

"No. It's more than that, Jaycee. That dream place is real—it's a projection of an actual physical situation. To survive there requires a heavy-duty spacesuit—which suggests that it's a very hot place. The gravity is only about half Terra-normal. It has an atmosphere—I could hear transmitted sounds. It also has a hydrosphere—I was floating on some of it. I didn't dream those things, Jaycee. They were communicated to me. It's an actual place—somewhere."

If it does exist it's in Messier thirty-one—right across the void. But I don't see why its existence is in any way important.

"It is, though. I've got to go there, Jaycee. That dream was a sample of visualized chaos. My journey down that tunnel is an already established part of future history.''

You've altered chaos trends before, Bron, so what makes this one immutable?

''Because all we've beaten out here is a few dozen individuals and an uncommonly antique spacefleet. The real enemy is still untouched and probably just as virulent as ever. If they could put a hellburner down on Onaris, they could as easily put one on Terra or any of the other prime worlds. In fact, those burners may already be on their way. If we're ever to win totally I have to carry the fight to them. And that dream, Jaycee, is a prediction of some part of the result of my doing just that.''

''Ananias, how many ships have you with the potential subspace capability to take them to Messier thirty-one?''

Ananias whistled as he caught the implications of the question. ''It's never been done, Bron. Not right across the void. The *Tantalus* went farther out than any vessel ever did before—and that was only a fraction of the distance.''

''This time I want to go right across. Give me details of any Commando ship with a known subspace-jump capability of better than ten kiloparsecs.''

''But you're talking about six hundred kiloparsecs. No ship has that capability.''

''No ship has attempted it, so we don't know. I want ships, as well as volunteer crews to man them. We've carried out a review of all Destroyer ships and we think we may have three with that sort of subspace potential. I'd prefer to have thirty."

"Engaged, Bron. I'll run a computer check immediately. If we've any candidates I'll let you know."

"Jaycee, are you there?"

No. Doc on-line. Deep-space Research Labs have just returned a verdict that there's barely a two percent possibility of any ship of known design reaching Messier thirty-one. After about fifteen kiloparsecs the subspace dropout determination becomes so imprecise that dropout probability approaches null infinity. There's no record of anything's having jumped more than fifteen kiloparsecs and having returned to real-space.

"At two percent possibility it's still a risk I'm prepared to take. If necessary we'll take the distance in a number of small jumps."

That won't help. You can't fix dropout coordinates in an area where there are no stars to use as reference points.

"We'll manage somehow, Doc. It's got to be done."

I still don't see what you expect to achieve if you get there. You can't take an army with you and the star population of Andromeda is even larger than that of our own galaxy. The odds are several hundred thousand million to one against your even locating the right primary, let alone the alien homeworld.

"I'm taking a chaos crew with me. It's estimated that we can get a fair chaos fix from examining the origins of the alien fleet. That should give us some idea of the sector. From there it will be a matter of making astronomical correction for galactic drift and rotation.''

You're in charge, Bron. If you want to try it we can't stop you. But from where we're sitting it seems a foolish waste of men and ships.

''Objection noted, Doc. But I have to play the game my way. Is Jaycee there?''

She's off duty. Want me to put out a call?

''No. Just describe her to me.''

You know I can't do that, Bron. You don't really expect an answer.

''I fail to see what's so damn secret about the description of someone who spends half her life practicing bitchiness inside my head.''

The information's secret for the specific reason that we don't want you to know. The two of you were psychologically paired to establish a strongly antagonistic relationship. As anticipated, you've achieved a high degree of rapport—one not complicated by common sentiment. It makes you two the best operating team we've got. That's why we won't allow anything to upset it.

Bron was amused. ''Like falling in love, for instance?''

Don't underestimate the power of the coupling between you two, Bron. You're more tightly keyed together, except physically, than two people could be in any normal relationship. You wouldn't get a weld that thorough even in a classic love match.

''Tell me more, Doc.''

I've told you too much already. From now on

*questions about Jaycee won't be answered. I just
wanted to show you how delicate the balance is.*

"I think you've shown me a whole lot more than
that. I think you've just reshaped a big piece of
future history."

Bron moved across the *Skua*'s bridge to a computer input terminal. His fingers sought their positions on the keyboard, but his eyes avoided watching what his fingers were conveying to the keys.
His gaze remained firmly fixed on the instruments
across the room.

*What are you doing, Bron? I think we ought to
have a record of that.*

"Stay out of my hair, Doc. This whole assignment's out of your control. Regardless of your
advice, I'm going to Messier thirty-one. And if I
survive I'm coming back to tackle the galaxy's
other great enigma."

And what the hell is that?

"Doc, I'm coming back for Jaycee. And it'll
take more than the Stellar Commando to stop
me."

Deftly, subtly, the thunder of the gravity drives
died and the six ships jumped into the dimensionless corridors of tachyon space. Every time they
reached the quiescent phase of a jump, Bron quit
the jump harness and began to plot more detail into
his new venture. The Destroyer corvette *Nemesis*
was only a fraction of the size of the *Skua*, but its
subspace installation was the most powerful in the
fleet. Alongside, but invisible now, two other Destroyer ships and three from the Commando fleet

sang their eerie way through the superluminal continuum.

Down in the hastily conceived chaos complex of the *Nemesis*, a volunteer crew of technicians worked steadily at the task of pin-pointing with increasing definition the origin of the alien armada. The grinning imp in charge of the fantastic improvisation was none other than Academician Laaris, formerly of the *Tantalus*, who presided with troll-like exhilaration over the most detailed and exacting chaos determination ever made.

Lacking the usual stars for subspace reference, the coordinates set up in the subspace grids were based on Laaris's increasingly hardening chaos values for the path of the alien fleet as he back-tracked it through space and time. Bron was keeping his fingers crossed. When setting up subspace coordinates, the use of theoretical chaos positions instead of a replica star matrix was a risky and untried procedure. So far the six ships had taken seven leaps of fifty thousand parsecs and had arrived virtually simultaneously and without incident. This was so far at variance with the statistical odds of such long-range subspace operations that all those involved were conscious of living on borrowed time.

It was Laaris who first noted a peculiarity in the chaos-predicted routing. Refusing to accept Bron as anything other than Haltern the master syncretist, he continually brought to him the most obscure chaos problems for explanation. Partly with Ander's help and partly from his own improv-

ing understanding of chaos mechanisms, Bron
usually managed to produce a satisfactory answer.
This time Laaris knew that he had found a problem
to end all chaos problems, and his delight at the
finding was equalled only by his concern for its
possible consequences.

"Mastership 'altern, this you 'ave to explain to
me." He unrolled a dozen chartstrips on the table
and waited with impatient expectancy while Bron
examined them in detail.

"What's the problem?" asked Bron.

"This divergence." Laaris indicated the computer comments running down the edge of the
strip. "The farther we go, the more our course
diverges from a straight line."

"Which surely only indicates that the path of the
alien fleet was similarly curved?"

"Not so! We should be proceeding down
straight coinciden' axis from resultant to origin.
This is a geocentric line—he got no damn right to
bend."

"What about the time factor?" asked Bron.
"With the rotation and drift of the Andromeda
galaxy through the years, surely our course must
curve as we backtrack the alien ships through
time. The best fix we can expect chaos to achieve
is the position of the point of origin as it was seven
hundred million years ago."

Laaris hopped from one foot to the other in
sheer exasperation.

"I already 'ave explained. Chaos axis always
straight line. You confuse it with space-time where
you can 'ave your curvature. In chaos all shock-

spheres are spherical and all axes straight. She don' work no other way."

Bron examined the chartstrips again, noting the computed tensorial factors thronging the margin of the record.

"Since it does appear axiomatic that all chaos axes are straight, while our course is not, the logical inference would seem to be that the factors we are feeding into our computers are not true chaos determinations."

"Do you doubt our detectors?" Laaris was immediately on the defensive.

"Of course not. I know you—and you would have checked them before you brought this to me. It's the entropic data itself that I suspect. How possible is it that we're being fed a signal our detectors find indistinguishable from the ripples of a real event?"

Laaris rubbed his brow. "It's only a question of signal strength. Any signal indistinguishable from a true event process would be handled as though it were an event process. If it swamped the original signal we might never know of substitution. Why you ask?"

"Because it has just occurred to me," said Bron, "that we perhaps aren't searching for the aliens—we're being led to them."

XX

"JAYCEE FIND ANDER. I need to know if deliberate entropic transmissions are feasible."

I've had Ander on-line since Laaris came to see you. He says modified entropic transmission techniques are both feasible and actually in use for instantaneous communications over galactic distances. In fact, a form of entropic transmission is used in the transfer link itself.

"Then we could be riding down some alien homing beam we are mistaking for an event axis?"

Affirmative, Bron. With their technology anythin' is possible.

The break-jump alert signaled termination of the present traverse through subspace, and shortly Bron was immersed in the intricate agonies of re-entry. A sudden encounter with a burst of startled alien goose-mutter filled him with apprehension. Since his induced coma aboard the *Skua* the voices had not been raised to a detectable level, though he always took anti-hypnotic drugs before he slept as an insurance against recurrence.

It took the ship's radio officer scant seconds to identify the attendant catastrophe. Two of their companion ships had failed to make the dropout. A slight possibility existed that the missing ships would revert to real-space at some point in the near future and in some place far removed from their intended destination. More probably they had joined that lost legion of ships doomed to spend forever in the weird, dimensionless corridors of the subspace mode.

Bron called a radio conference of his ships' captains while the next jump was being programed. At their present rate, four more subspace jumps of fifty kiloparsecs each were required to complete the journey to the fringes of the Andromeda galaxy. Each jump bore its own possibility of failed dropout. The statistical odds of survival had already been stretched heavily. Bron decided to try the last two hundred kiloparsecs in one jump. Nobody dissented, though they all knew that they were playing in an area of physics where they had no qualifications whatever.

Laaris soon produced evidence of a pure entropic transmission of such an intensity that it completely obliterated his normal chaos determinations. Although the trap was now painfully obvious, Bron ordered the indicated route to be set up in the subspace grids. Where there was an alien beacon, he reasoned, there also would be the most likely place to find aliens. All coordinates were double- and triple-checked, and the four ships jumped into subspace.

When she finally reached the dropout point, the *Nemesis* was alone.

Bron had to admit to curiously mixed feelings as his lone craft hit real-space at the edge of the great galaxy of Andromeda. Fear, anxiety and regret for the loss of his companion ships were paramount, but wonder was not the least of his emotions. He had ranged broadly through the Milky Way and knew something of the infinite variety of its stars. Superficially these stars in Andromeda were of similar range in size, type, spectrum and density of distribution. Yet never could his own eyes have convinced him that these were the stars of home. In some indefinable way the magnificent array seemed ineffably unique and foreign.

Perhaps Andromeda indeed was different— among all the stars and planets in the Milky Way only Terra had detectably produced intelligent life. Now, on the edge of another galaxy, he was destined to meet the alien equivalent of Man. His fleet now trimmed to a solitary ship by precalculated circumstance, he knew that when he came around that last bend in the tunnel he would be both defenseless and alone. Alone before a life form that had acquired space capability back when the first alarms of life had begun to shrill on Terra.

"Listen, you out there," he said, suddenly struck by the thought that the aliens probably could intercept his transfer link. "I know you're listening."

The goose-mutter rose to audibility, then descended again below threshold value, almost as if in answer.

Bron continued, "I'm coming down to meet you. You've destroyed many of our worlds without apparent reason. If I wanted I could destroy many more of yours, since I have access to ships that can cross the void in mere fractions of a lifetime. Therefore I come out of strength, not out of weakness. I shall not bear weapons, but if I or my ship comes to harm the rest of my kind will know of it and you will be destroyed because of it."

Again the goose-mutter rose like the waves of an angry sea, then hushed to a background noise like surf on a distant shore.

Laaris came in with his latest calculations. He was now able to pinpoint the source of entropic noise. It appeared to originate from a system only two kiloparsecs in from the alien Rim. Bron authorized the jump and, after the computers had run an astronomical survey to establish a true replica star matrix, the *Nemesis* slid into subspace on her terminal jump.

It emerged in the vicinity of a perfectly ordinary K5 primary of about eighty percent of the mass of Sol. It had only one planet, which was smaller than

Terra. Telescopic examination of what little could be seen of the planet's surface revealed nothing significant. It was a craggy rock-ball, cloud-bound, apparently lifeless, and with a boiling and turbulent hydrocarbon atmosphere. The temperature of its surface was in excess of two hundred degrees Celsius. The alien entropic signal was originating from some region of the unfriendly terrain, but the limited discrimination of the jury-rigged scanners on the *Nemesis* failed to resolve the location except in the broadest terms.

The *Nemesis* carried only one scoutcraft, a pinnace. Bron ordered heavy-duty spacesuits to be broken out and called for two volunteers to accompany him. The volunteers came readily. When Bron inspected the suit with which he had been provided, he knew that his journey down that dreadful tunnel was all too soon to become reality.

Having been built primarily for deep-space work, the pinnace was unhappy in any kind of atmosphere. It proved especially so in the vapor-laden hydrocarbon storms it now entered. Unable to use its thrust motors efficiently at such low speeds and having an inadequate aerodynamic form for achieving stability in boiling multi-fractioned mineral-oil vapors, the craft stalled, balked and was buffeted by sidewinds, convection currents and wax-laden down-draughts.

Occasionally, through a hail of platelets of crystalline higher-paraffin snow, Bron saw the surface of the planet. He gazed with amazement at the vicious rocky crags swept by an oily, droplet-loaded wind and at the sullen swell of a liquid metal sea. The land masses were spitefully fragmented, broken islands and torn peaks reflecting the atrocious vehemence of unearthly Nature. Here and there vast mountain ranges seemed to have been torn out by the roots and tossed sideways to shatter into razor-sharp rocks and black, impenetrable fissures. Nowhere was there any sign of the restoration of order that would indicate intelligent intervention.

Bron and his volunteers made three sorties in the pinnace, returning to the *Nemesis* to rest, recalibrate their instruments and discharge their records for processing. Laaris was operating all the computer power he had at his command, trying to equate the varying alien signal strength with some aspect of the geometry of the planet. The information from their low-level flights was beginning to match up to a pattern of coincidences, indicating at first a point on the southern hemisphere, then gradually tightening to a particular land mass and finally to coordinates indicating an area a bare kilometer in diameter.

Bron called for aerial photographs and both high- and low-level sets were matched to give a reasonable facsimile of the area. Bron's hands were shaking as he took the finished prints. Some alien description of the place he had not admitted to his consciousness suddenly burst into recognition. He knew instinctively how to interpret the patterns of light and darkness. He realized that all this had been described to him in the deep hypnotic coma he had experienced on the *Skua*. On his awakening he had remembered only the traumatic moments leading to the point where he had been torn away from the encounter just before the climax. Now he was back at the beginning of the journey—and this time he felt sure he was destined to go right through to the end.

"Jaycee!"

Readin' you, Bron.

"Give me a readout of the secondary circuits on the transfer link."

Why? You thinkin' of takin' a holiday?

"I said read them, Jaycee."

Very well. Catatonic Withdrawal. Anesthesia with Maintained Consciousness, Punishment, Death. What you meanin', Bron?

Bron held up a print and pointed to a shadowed area that bore no detail.

"That's the entrance to the tunnel, Jaycee. I'm going down there. Unless I miss my guess it's going to be a rough journey. You've got six hours to prepare. Get some rest. Once we start, I'll be needing all the back-up you can give me."

XXI

THE PINNACE MADE a precarious touchdown on the only available flat space in the area. The landing was a classic example of triumph over bitter odds. All the way down through the troposphere, the heavy methane winds had buffeted the craft and repeatedly sent it keeling dangerously off course. Storm-walls—sheets of condensing hydrocarbon polymers—wrapped themselves around the optical navigation systems and made nonsense of the readings of the laser altimeters. The embarrassingly high charge of static the pinnace had acquired had to be carefully bled away with sodium plasma before the craft dared approach closely the eutectic metal sea.

Finally, however, the landing was achieved. Flexing slightly on its cushioned legs under the pressures of the storm, the craft stood with nose pointed longingly toward the quietude of space. Its carefully chosen position was atop a black flat-topped rock that protruded like a miniature island from the dull metallic sea. From the incidence of surrounding rocks it was obvious that the ocean here was actually no more than the fringes of a tide eroding a broken coastal shelf.

The sweeping metal surf hammered the black rock with an inertial insistence unnerving to contemplate. The shock of the wave impact was easily felt inside the shuddering ship. A tide with a density of eight, and a temperature of two hundred degrees Celsius, was no mean wash.

A hundred meters away, a mountain cavern opened like a black mouth in a twisted misshapen head. By some mechanism yet to be explained, a strong tidal current entered the cavern but was subject to no apparent reverse of flow. Whatever entered the dark galleries tended to remain.

Your aptitude for most of the weaknesses of the flesh is proven beyond doubt. Jaycee was darkly critical. *Unfortunately your capacity for successful suicide has never yet been established. Is that the place?*

"We know the signals are coming from this area

and the stream entering the cave seems to equate with the dream."

So what do you plan to do?

"I'm going in there, Jaycee."

With a task force?

"No. Just me, with you along."

I don't get your motive, Bron. It's a suicide trip even without aliens. Look at the strength of that current. What you tryin' to prove?

"My journey down there is already part of history. I have to know what's beyond that last bend."

Level with me, Bron. You're no martyr and you're not riskin' your fool neck in the interests of interstellar relationships. It isn't heroism and it's not just idle curiosity. You're too damn egotistic and self-centered to care about the rest of the universe. If you're going down that tunnel it's because you've a pretty good idea there's something you think you want at the end of it and you're reasonably sure you're goin' to be able to take it with you. I can't see how you figure it, but as sure as hell I'm curious.

"You know what your trouble is, Jaycee? You've got no soul."

And you know what your trouble is, Bron? You're runnin' remarkably short of future.

Bron watched the fearful scene for many minutes before he before he began to make his move. At last he quit the pinnace. The terrifying pressures outside stiffened the heat resistant suit and made it even more cumbersome, especially since he had to walk across the broken rocks above the tide-race without being able properly to see the areas to which he committed his feet.

His journey through the terrible atmosphere was like that of a deep-sea diver caught in some undersea vortex. It was a moot point as to whether his own volition or the barbarous physics of the place was most responsible for taking him into the entrance to the cave, but he had a distinct feeling that even the wind was conspiring to make him enter.

Keep goin', Bron. I'm ridin' with you. Jaycee's voice was a welcome touch of reality in the nightmare.

"How are the life-support systems doing, Jaycee?"

The suit appears adequate for about ten hours if you don't damage it. We're not as certain that you can stand that length of confinement. If you get claustrophobic you'll likely do yourself some damage.

"You know how to quiet me if I get that bent."

It would be a pleasure—and not for the first time. You always were a psychological mess. Her words carried the edge of disgust.

He was well inside the cavern mouth now, trying to use the suit's inbuilt lighting to define his way. The jet-black of the rock refused to throw back any useful definition and only the racing metal stream showed up as a wide, glittering tide under a roof that progressively lowered toward an enigmatic somewhere.

Then he heard it. The goose-mutter, this time coming via the suit phones, not the transfer link. From somewhere impossibly far away he could hear the glutinous cries and knew from their urgency that they had detected his coming. He also heard Jaycee draw a sharp breath of anxiety.

Shortly he was forced to stop. The jagged bank on which he had been painfully clambering came to an end with the gradual closing of the tunnel's mouth. Experimentally he tested the racing stream, hoping to strike bottom, but such was its depth and density that he was unable to apply sufficient weight to force his foot down to the underlying rock. As if he had extended his leg into a torrent of quicksilver, the heavy liquid drag tore him loose from the precarious handholds and with a cry he slipped and fell on his back into the eutectic tide.

As he fell he heard the headlamp strike a spiteful point of rock. This should not have been able to damage the lamp, but somehow it caused it to cease its solid-state illumination. For the first time since he had entered the tunnel he experienced panic as a full appreciation of his animal helplessness closed about his thinking. He was being carried face-up along this fantastic tunnel that murmured and whispered with the ripple and eddy of the unalterable metal flood.

Are you all right, Bron?

Her voice brought back objectivity. "I'm still afloat—if you're awarding any points for buoyancy. But that's about the sum of my assets at this point."

263

Believe me, you're not jokin'. Aliens or no aliens, you know you've got no chance of ever gettin' back out of there. So precisely what you up to, Bron?

"Would you believe that I'm not up to anything?"

No! I know you for the scheming wretch you are.

"Then I'll tell you what's on my mind. I'm accepting that dream imagery as being a piece of visualized chaos. I regard it as proof that I did—will—somehow penetrate right into this place. Right up to the point where the aliens are."

But you don't know what happens beyond that point.

"No, except that it's axiomatic that this expedition must be successful."

Where in space did you conjure that piece of wishful thinking?

"My dear Jaycee, it's been implicit in everything the aliens have done. The hellburners, the armada, were all in some way aimed at lessening the probability of this contact's ever being made. All those years ago they tried to avert the happening that is soon to take place. They would scarcely have gone to those lengths to prevent something that was going to fail anyway. Therefore it has to succeed."

I don't see it that way, Bron. I think they've tried every way they know to destroy the chaos factor you represent. All their long-range attacks failed because of miscalculation, so they've induced you to come to them. I think you're in a one-way chaos disposal unit. As I read it, they've got you in a trap that will become increasingly lethal until the chaos potential you represent is utterly destroyed.

"I don't agree, Jaycee. But even if you're right, they've already failed."

What you meanin', Bron?

"A point you and they may have overlooked. I'm not just an individual. Through the transfer link I'm a composite being, a gestalt synthesis of me, you, your computing and communications complex and such characters as Doc, Ander and Ananias. The aliens might destroy me, but the rest of the gestalt remains with all the original knowledge and purpose untouched. Get yourself a new agent and nothing has been lost but a few kilos of replaceable protein. You see, it isn't just me who's the catalyst, but the whole system of which I happen to be a part."

Quit talkin', Bron. I'm turnin' up the audio gain. Sounds like a waterfall or rapids ahead. What's the current like?

"Seems to be pulling harder, but there's not much I can judge it by."

See if you can strike a bank and wedge on it. Accordin' to our instruments, that fall ahead is really vicious.

"How vicious?"

We could be well adrift because we don't know the full range of physical parameters, but we're readin' a probable drop approachin' three kilometers.

"Jaycee—"

Yes?

"Nothing. What are the chances of surviving that?"

If you were a jelly I'd rate the prospect at one percent. However, as a vertebrate—

"Will the suit hold?"

Depends what you hit. Most probably not. Some of the life-support systems won't stand that sort of deceleration anyway.

He felt a bump. In an agonized reappraisal of the sensations that reached his cocooned form he knew he was in free fall and plunging through a dark hiatus that seemed to be limited only by eternity. From somewhere far below, the angry sound of violently agitated fluids rushed up to meet him. Unashamedly he screamed and, as he continued to fall, the scream became frozen on his lips.

Sick spite of a broken body . . . He felt the slight motion of the wash lifting and falling.

. . . *cryin' futility unto a futile wind* . . .

The sense of being borne on a moving current down a dark tunnel. Perceptible changes of direction, unseen, felt through some inertial function. The quick lap of the dark stream being echoed spitefully from the pressing span above. And sounds—mucilaginous, coagulating, curdled, clammy sounds. Sounds that chilled the blood.

. . . *the mind mazed not by the searin' steel, the nibblin' nerve* . . .

Somewhere a glutinous goose sang a solitary anserine hymn through a throat filled with its own life-blood. It was joined by another and yet others in an inhuman anthem distilled from terror and corrodingly bitter reproaches.

Overhead, the pressures of seven hundred million years of evolution leaned against the tunneled rock. His lungs were refusing to accept the tainted, metal-tasting air and he could hear his own sweat dripping about his ears. The inability to feel or move his arms and legs brought him quickly to the verge of hysteria. Another bend and this time he clearly felt the bump against the bank . . . felt the bump . . . on his suit.

"Jaycee—"

Ridin' with you, Bron.

"The fall didn't kill me, then?"

We threw you into catatonic shock. You went down easier that way. Actually it wasn't quite as bad as we thought. The height was broken by a cascade of about seventeen falls. You're about three kilometers deep now and the level is still fallin'. We've got you under conscious anesthesia at the moment because we didn't know how badly you may have been mashed by the falls.

"Lift the anesthesia, I'd like to find out."

A transparent hum filled his head for a moment, then painful feeling flooded into his limbs.

How you feelin', Bron?

"Doubt if I've an unstrained joint anywhere, but nothing seems to be broken."

Apparently the suit was becomin' more rigid as the depth-pressure increased. It's more of a casin' now. Talk about the devil lookin' after his own!

"Can you hear the aliens, Jaycee?"

We've been plottin' sound intensities. Accordin' to our calculations you're goin' to be meetin' them in about seven minutes.

The goose-mutter grew into a vast, brassy braying, a throbbing crescendo of sound that struck

267

back from the tunnel walls in a rippled anacamptic roar. The scolding choir was now so near that he felt he was almost in its midst. Another bump and he knew he had rounded the last of the dreadful bends. This time he was in no dream. There was no possibility of recall from the edge of nightmare.

This was reality.

He felt the stream slacken and heard echoes become attenuated by distance, as though he had entered a larger cavern. And then came light, a dim luminescence, straight glowing bars along level walls—and a sudden terrifying silence.

His back came to rest against an inclined tracery grille in which he found he could catch his heel and force himself up out of the eutectic sluice. He looked about him in dim amazement, warily prepared to meet his persecutors, no matter how terrible their form. But he found he was shockingly alone.

The metallic stream ran between straight and artificial banks, interrupted only by the fret on which he had laboriously climbed. Looking about, he found himself in a vast chamber whose distant and complex walls were covered by a thousand unguessable patterns that might have been either decorative or functional. Tall machines lurked like mute watchers in alcoves, the designs of which were mind-wrenching in the unearthly tenets of their forms. The machines were huge, silent and completely alien to him in purpose and concept. They were frightening in their strangeness.

He froze in horror at a movement from within the ranks of dark and unknown mechanisms. A familiar and plaintive cry rang out and chilled him to the marrow. Alien living shapes, dark in the sparse light, goose-stepped out from some unanticipated place and moved in profiled files—deliberately to the stream to drink.

He watched them curve horny bills incuriously into the metal stream—and just as incuriously waddle past his silent form, protesting some unknown indignity but oblivious to his presence. With mounting horror and increasing comprehension, he watched them go—degenerate, blind, ugly, leathery, alien and completely stupid quasi-aviforms—they nested, fed and presumably bred in this treasurehouse of a lost culture. Even their prehensile hands had atrophied in favor of a broad bill and a long, thrusting neck.

The whole chamber had the feeling of a cathedral—but in honor of what dead gods? There were a million clues but no answers. Bron realized the irony and incongruity of the announcing choir of voices. Once their hymns had held much meaning. Now their race neared an evolutionary end and their personal complaint had dwindled from cosmic considerations to a local spat about the infrequency of worms. While an alien phonograph had piped something from the pinnacle of their once-held greatness . . .

With returning confidence Bron started to explore. Some of the mechanisms had strange lights playing inside them, the luminescence even yet moving as though to perform some intelligent function even though the whole place was possessed by the stamp of incredible age. One machine, as he approached it, began to speak in a welter of the familiar goose-mutter, but softly, as if its resigned and sibilant speech were now a message of acquiescence, an apology for its previous paeans of hate. He regarded it uneasily, sensing that it was conscious of his presence and knowing that this was the voice that had menaced his dreams and probably directed the attack detail of the alien fleet. Now the machine acknowledged his mastery, but he felt no sense of triumph.

Where are the aliens, Bron?

"The kind we came to meet don't exist anymore, Jaycee. They're extinct."

But they attacked us!

"The far ancestors of these creatures did, but they faded and forgot us many millions of years ago. Perhaps there were a few live carcasses in the fleet, but they had long since lost their sense of purpose. Only machines carried out that nearly mindless battle."

How can you be so sure the aliens don't exist?

"Evolution, Jaycee. The fact that they achieved intelligence is a proof that they were evolving organisms. It took only about four million years for man to swing out of the trees and boost himself into space. With the possibility of that rate of progress, have you any idea where a further six hundred and ninety-six million years might take us? One thing is certain, we'll no longer be the dominant Homo sapiens. The same thing will have happened to us as has already happened to these aliens."

I hadn't thought of us that way.

"The development of intelligence is a kind of evolutionary critical reaction. It's unstable. The usefulness of intelligence as a long-term survival factor is questionable. It's probably not valid for much over five million years."

But what about the entropic beacon that brought you here?

"The aliens' ancestors made good machines, Jaycee—designed them to last an eternity, probably not realizing they would have forgotten how to use them long before the machines wore out. It's possible the beacon was their own deep-space communications link, or perhaps it was set up by some latter-day alien philosopher to invite anyone with the technology and competence to come and partake of the things they left behind. A sort of final memorial. This place—what is it? Some kind of museum designed to demonstrate their technological peak to any life form with the intelligence and the ability to gain admission."

But why did they send the armada and the hellburners?

"That's easily explained. Early in their evolution this place may have been something special to them. Then they read through their version of chaos analysis that one day an alien creature would stand in their special hall and pick it clean like a robber at a grave. Not realizing they would ultimately welcome the approach, they did all in their power to stop it. But whatever they did, that creature still remained, a positive future specter. They didn't know that their own failure—and not we—would destroy them."

271

You suspected all this before you went into the cavern, didn't you? Jaycee began to read new meanings into Bron's insistence on finding the alien homeworld.

"I knew they couldn't survive their own evolution over such a great period of time. Despite the apparent evidence to the contrary, there couldn't still be a functioning alien menace. Therefore there had to be something else."

And that's the thing you were after?

"Jaycee, these people were technologically far in advance of us in a great many fields. They could engineer molecules in the same way that we engineer machines. They used entropy as competently as we use electromagnetism. Imagine a fusion of their science with ours. Is there anything in the universe that would be denied us?"

And it all belongs to Bron! Jaycee's bitterness etched every syllable with acid.

"That's right, Jaycee. One day I'm coming back with enough men and equipment to open up this place and carry away as much of it as we have the ability to understand."

Someone may go back, Bron, but it won't be you. You've less than three hours' air left in that suit. Do you really think you stand a chance of getting out of there alive?

"Jaycee, there has to be a way out, for the same reason that there was a way in. All I need is sufficient intelligence to find it in time."

On the far side of the chamber he chanced upon a vast transparent tank. It was filled with a liquid whose misty blueness was haunting. His attention caught, he studied it more carefully, noting the myriad pinpoints of light that burned briefly and randomly through the faint haze. Occasionally he detected a slight trail between the flickering events and realized that he was watching an alien analogue of Ander's model of chaos. This was the Rosetta stone that could bridge two completely alien cultures. Its discovery was probably the most potentially important entropic event in history. If he could grasp its use the science of physics would be reborn.

He gazed with fascination into the misty field of the fluid, wondering if this were a model of the actual universe and if it operated in realtime. If so—one of those bright sparks might well represent himself. One particularly bright flare long illuminated a whole corner of the tank, but whether this had significance he would probably never know. He had two-and-a-half hours of air left and no obvious way to get out.

Finding the planet, entering the chamber via the cavern, comprehending the nature of what he had found—all struck Bron as tests to determine the qualifications of those who sought what the chamber contained. The last test was to get out alive. Since he had passed the others it seemed logical to him that, given the right facilities and the right knowledge, the last was also achievable. Except that here his facilities were nil and his knowledge was precariously slight. This test was perhaps designed to measure the assets of the individual and, with his failing air supply, it carried a barbarous time penalty. The aliens were choosing their successors with meticulous care.

He turned away from the tank, confident in the certainty that a way out had to exist. All he had to do was find it. To go back against the stream was impossible. Equally, at a depth of better than three kilometers and with a dwindling supply of air, he had no hope that those he had left on the surface would be able to get down to him in time. Perhaps after all, this was a one-way disposal unit.

Bron! Jaycee's voice came in with a sudden burst of alarm. *What's Cana doin' with his task force?*

"Exactly what I asked him to, I hope."

Antares reports a Destroyer task force in close orbit. Did you order that?

"Stay off my back, Jaycee. I've got worries enough as it is."

He returned to the study of his problem. The metallic stream moved on beyond the grille and fell smoothly into the bowels of the planet. No escape seemed possible by that route.

Bron. A dozen Destroyer heavy cruisers are enterin' the solar system and Space Defense reports another fifty on the way. Does Cana reckon on attackin' Terra?

Bron ignored her. His searchings had taken him back toward the middle of the chamber. The centerpiece was a broad and featureless pillar rising up to and probably into the solid roof. It was unique among the exhibits in its lack of complexity. In its base was a simple hatch opening internally and the sheer solidity of the tubular walls made him speculate as to what sort of pressures the structure was made to contain.

Bron, will you listen to me, damn you?

"I'm listening, Jaycee."

I know your brand of chaos. I'd recognize it anywhere. Did you order the destruction of the Antares base?

"Not its destruction, Jaycee—only its capture."

I guessed it. But why?

"It handles the transfer link. If I have Antares, Terra has lost control over me."

You won't get away with it, Bron. This is treason and you can't hope to win. The Stellar Commando will beat Cana clean out of space.

"The main Commando fleet is out with Ananias. Try telling that to him."

The singular simplicity of the pillar set it radically apart from the rest of the mechanisms and he could see now that its central position made it difficult to miss. The contrasts pointed to its enjoying some significance, the recognition of which transcended any mere differences in physiology or origin of knowledge. It was something designed to appeal uniquely to sheer intelligence, however derived.

For the first time since he had entered the cavern Bron permitted himself to smile.

Damn you! Damn you! Jaycee's vehemence cut like a white-hot knife. *You've got this all sewn up, haven't you? Ananias has taken the Commando fleet so far out into the void that we can't contact it by normal FTL radio. Our only chance is by transfer link to the Intelligence Radioship—*

"—and Ananias has control of that." Bron finished the sentence for her. "Let's face it, Jaycee, Terran dominance is finished."

You're goin' to destroy Terra? Her voice rose high with incredulity.

"Quite the contrary. I need her—and the other prime worlds. But in their proper perspective. Not as fumbling imperial powers, but as members of a total union of inhabited planets. It's all part of the agreement between Ananias and Cana. Terra, her Rim Dependencies and the planets of the Destroyer Federation, are going to be welded into one entity. Terra isn't going to like it, but that's the way history has to go. There's too much space to conquer for mankind to be divided."

He turned and entered the shaft, examining the hatch. It had a simple pressure device to hold it shut. If there were alien instructions regarding its use, he could not discern them, but he moved now with the blind faith that its function was what logic claimed it to be. He closed the hatch behind him.

Immediately a rush of liquid metal swirled about his feet and began to lift and raise him bodily up the shaft. Higher and higher the wave lifted him until he began to think that the shaft was limitless and that by some trick of physics he would continue to rise forever. Only the occasional brush of his suit against the black encasement assured him that he was still moving upward.

Bron, Antares has surrendered and landing parties are being set down. That makes you a traitor. Do you know of any reason why I shouldn't press the murder button?

"If you feel you want to you'll have to be quick,

276

Jaycee. The first task of that landing party is to destroy the transfer-link aerials. But if you fail—do you know what's going to happen? I'll be coming back to Terra specifically for you—and regardless of the cost. I've acquired one hell of an empire, and when the task of running it becomes a little rough—believe me, I'm going to need all the help I can get. Don't tell me the role of First Lady of the Universe is something that doesn't appeal?"

You know what you are, Bron—you're a Godlost egotistical louse.

"I figure that makes us two of a kind, Jaycee. As I begin to recall it, you're sort of damned yourself."

Finally there came a change, almost undetectable among the poor sensations that reached inside the suit. Something akin to an instinct warned him that he had reached his destination. Initially nothing appeared to be different. Then, on searching carefully, he noticed faint points of light overhead. In a shock of reorientation he knew that he was looking at the stars. Somewhere, one of those points of light was the galaxy of the Milky Way and he was floating on his back on a flooding rock-pool of liquid metal under the stillness of an alien night.

He switched on the suit's radio beacon and, while he waited for the pinnace to arrive, looked about at the starry pointers of his new empire. And a woman's sobbing heard from six hundred thousand parsecs reminded him that he was a creature with human weaknesses as well as special strengths. Somehow nothing was ever going to be quite the same again.

FRITZ LEIBER

ISAAC ASIMOV